■ □ ■ □ ■

THE GRAND PRIZE
AND O   STORIES

Writings from an Unbound Europe

■ □ ■ □ ■

DANIELA CRĂSNARU

THE GRAND PRIZE
AND OTHER STORIES

Edited and translated from the Romanian
by Adam J. Sorkin with the author

NORTHWESTERN UNIVERSITY PRESS

EVANSTON, ILLINOIS

Northwestern University Press
Evanston, Illinois 60208-4170

Printed in the United States of America

10 9 8 7 6 5 4 3 2 1

ISBN 0-8101-1849-1 (cloth)
ISBN 0-8101-1850-5 (paper)

Library of Congress Cataloging-in-Publication Data

Crăsnaru, Daniela
    [Marele premiu. English]
    The grand prize and other stories / Daniela Crăsnaru ; edited and translated from
the Romanian by Adam J. Sorkin with the author.
        p. cm. — (Writings from an unbound Europe)
    ISBN 0-8101-1849-1 (cloth text : alk. paper) — ISBN 0-8101-1850-5 (trade paper
alk. paper)
    1. Crăsnaru, Daniela—Translations into English. I. Title: Grand prize and other
stories. II. Sorkin, Adam J. III. Title. IV. Series.
PC840.13.R34M313 2004
859'.334—DC22

                                                                            2004004724

The paper used in this publication meets the minimum requirements of the American
National Standard for Information Sciences—Permanence of Paper for Printed Library
Materials, ANSI Z39.48-1992.

■ □ ■ □ ■

CONTENTS

■ □ ■ □ ■

ACKNOWLEDGMENTS

Grateful acknowledgment is made to the editors of the following journals, in which some of the stories in this book first appeared: *International Quarterly* ("The European Mechanism"), *Orient Express* ("About Happiness"), *Southerly* ("The Giraffe"), and *TriQuarterly* ("The Grand Prize").

Both Daniela Crăsnaru and Adam J. Sorkin express gratitude to the Rockefeller Foundation, which provided parallel residencies at the Foundation's Study Center in Bellagio, Italy, during the summer of 1995, with additional assistance for Daniela Crăsnaru from the Roberto Celli Memorial Fund. Without this support, the initial translation of this collection of stories would not have happened.

Adam J. Sorkin likewise wishes to express appreciation to Penn State University for its generous support through the College of Liberal Arts, the Institute for the Arts and Humanistic Studies, the Center for Russian and East European Studies, and the Delaware County Campus. Thanks to Ethel Rackin, who gave these stories the benefit of an expert reading. And finally, thanks to Nancy Sorkin for her patient, repeated, careful reading of the manuscript, her sound advice, and her good cheer when the translators stormed at one another in usually sunny Italy.

■ □ ■ □ ■

THE GRAND PRIZE
AND OTHER STORIES

ABOUT HAPPINESS

IT WAS, AS THEY SAY, A HAPPY FAMILY. OR WHAT WE'VE LEARNED TO believe a happy family is, happiness being in our common dictionary something rather vaguely defined, an imprecise but luminous notion, something good, indeed very good, which only the reckless or hypercritical try to pick apart, to inspect its every facet, and then the result is more amazing than anyone thought possible. Amazing in what way? Well, let's leave that to the reckless, compulsive people we've already mentioned.

They married while students at the university and lived for a few years with her parents, Doina's. The first year after they both got jobs, Michael appeared. A young family with a normal child, that is to say, full of promise, with no health problems, no job worries, no social difficulties, with neither ridiculous ambitions nor terrible frustrations leading to anguish, and without any kind of spectacular rise giving cause for envy or precipitous fall followed by false commiserations. That is to say, everything bright, auspicious, and—why not?—pretty. A family that most parents would desire for their children.

After some time passed, Doina decided to go on for further education, Liviu registered for his doctorate, and Michael managed to pronounce successfully the hated sound *rrr.*

Shopping, cooking, theater and movie tickets, Sundays at the stadium, the Ferris wheel, the zoo, animated cartoons, visits to Aunt Sophie, the libraries of the institute and the academy, taking notes, caramel cream—mmm, a treat—Monopoly with Dana, Doru, Radu, and Marica, enthusiasm, élan, and energy, economy of energy, one beer, two, all of life before you. All of life, all of life.

At least this is the way it was perceived by Mrs. Lisandru, their neighbor (almost nothing escapes her watchful eyes), and by Aunt Sophie, although she lives far away in the Encampments Road district, and even by us, from here, from our particular angle—which doesn't mean that likewise it's our point of view.

They found an apartment, and, after a while, helped by friends, because, of course, they had friends, too, they moved there. A three-room apartment very close to the North Station. Directly across from it. They settled themselves in, and, as might be expected, very soon they felt quite comfortable in their new home.

One winter evening, coming home from the library almost frozen (the doctoral work was progressing slowly but surely), Liviu Georgescu found a scribbled note on his refrigerator: *Liviu, dear, I'm at the hairdresser's. Radu and Marica are stopping by this evening. Please buy bread. Doina.* Liviu looked at his watch and realized that no shop in the neighborhood would still be open at that hour. Well, that's the way it is. They'll eat without bread. OK, potatoes instead. And he searched in the pantry for potatoes. He had already placed them neatly on the kitchen table and was feeling among the dull knives for the sharpest one when the door opened and, from the threshold, Doina's voice: "Hi, did you buy the bread?"

"I just got home, and look how late it is. They've closed."

"But in the station? Did you try the restaurant there?"

"No. I didn't think of it."

"Well, you see, darling, you see! So please hurry, darling, because they're coming at about half past eight and I'd like to make hot sandwiches."

Liviu Georgescu put on his coat and went out. He crossed the tram tracks, scrounged through his pocket for some small change to buy a ticket to enter the station, and headed straight to the station restaurant.

A big crowd, luggage, the standard recorded musical tones that signaled a train's coming or going, and the loudspeakers' artificial voice announcing arrivals and departures. "Intercity 836 for Constanţa departs in five minutes. Persons who accompanied travelers on board the train are requested to leave now."

He stood transfixed for some seconds, rooted to the spot, anticipating the repetition of this announcement as if it had been addressed to him. Then he tried to make his way through the crowd but again stopped short, right in front of a group of young people carrying skis and passing around a bottle of vodka, laughing and chatting loudly. Liviu Georgescu had never been skiing. And for more than ten years, since his second year at the university, he had not taken a train. In fact he never went anywhere. In summers during their vacation, they used to travel to Uncle Viorel's in the mountain resort of Breaza, borrowing Aunt Sophie's car. But since he'd started his doctorate, Liviu stayed home to work in the library during his time off while Doina left with Michael for the Black Sea coast. Just think, to be living so close to the railroad station and not to go away anywhere, he said to himself entering the restaurant. Merely to buy bread—for this to be all the station's good for! What a curious thing. And with the loaf of bread under his arm, he suddenly found himself borne on a wave of people surging to track 5, where the Orient Express was arriving from Vienna. He found himself at the end of the line of people for track 5, waiting together with the others for the outpouring from the train. He stood on tiptoe to see better. To see whom? Nobody. Just to see. And as the crowd flowed past him, he recalled his first trip to Bucharest as a boy of four, a very sickly boy. At a shop called The Three Little Bears, his parents bought him ice skates and an outfit with a colorful appliqué of a man skiing, and next they went somewhere near the center of the city to a photographer who took a lot of pictures. Then he—a child who wasn't ever allowed to run, to work up a sweat—after he had been taken to two doctors, he was handed the skates, and his mother cried and said, "From now on you can do anything you like, my little Liviu, Mama's lost lamb." Years later he would find out that those doctors had decided he couldn't be saved. But two years of penicillin, isoniazid, and PAS restored him to health.

And while he was heading for the exit with the bread under his arm, a little bit confused and, who knows why, shivering slightly, there also came back to his mind the roll with butter that he'd eaten on the train to Bușteni when he was five, the first time he allowed himself to eat a buttered roll. Generally he ate almost nothing, he lived on air, as his mother said; this buttered roll had been given to him by a little girl maybe one or two years older. What was her name? He'd forgotten, although a couple of years after this train trip, his mother had remarked at dinner how neatly she'd eaten on that train (and mentioned her name). Do you still recall how good that roll with butter was? The girl had black eyes, very black, and black hair, and he dreamed of her several times and was almost certain he would see her again. Where? On a train, of course. He continually asked his mother, pestering her again and again, Aren't we going anywhere by train, Mama? No, my pet, not for the time being. Everywhere throughout the first train he'd gone on after that, to another resort, he looked for the girl, but she wasn't to be found. Her not being on the train seemed incredible to him, and he cried and cried. Why are you crying, Mama's little man? What's wrong, my dear boy? Does something hurt? No, no, no, through his sobs. No, no, no.

Look at the nonsense that pops into his head after so long, what babble. The station clock already showed a quarter to nine. God, how long he's shilly-shallied here, like a nitwit! Doina will be upset. Worse, maybe their guests will have arrived.

Beginning with that evening when he went to buy bread at the station restaurant, Liviu Georgescu avoided the station as much as he could. It was a place he felt must be steered clear of. Why? As long as he felt himself, and surely was, self-controlled and levelheaded, an ordinary person with a calm and untroubled life, with no nagging discontent, we could say from every possible perspective he had no reason for fear.

After some time, he told himself this was pure stupidity and deliberately went to the station to buy newspapers. Next to buy some aspirin from the pharmacy in the station. Next bread sticks. Next . . .

"You're so late. Where have you been, Liviu?"

"Well, I wandered through the station. Why are you asking?"

"Just because . . . I don't know. But it seems nearly every single day you find some reason to go to the station. Is there somebody you're waiting for?"

"Whom would I be waiting for, darling? What are you talking about?"

And in fact, what had he done wrong? What was unusual in this? He mingled with the crowd, he felt immersed in the fever of departure. He would choose a train scheduled to leave, let's say, in half an hour, look for the platform, wait for the train to pull in, join the people weighed down by their luggage, and feel free as he walked along, his hands thrust casually in his pockets.

Only after the train had started to leave and he saw the last car disappearing into the distance would he feel a knot in his throat, a mild sense of being torn apart, a hot spasm of bitterness.

Soon he decided to devote himself to trains that were departing. The ones that arrived meant nothing to him because Liviu Georgescu wasn't waiting for anyone.

But he didn't do this all day every day, no, good God, no. Once a week, or maybe twice. He was perfectly rational, perfectly the master of himself, there was nothing unnatural in what he did. He had discovered a pleasure that didn't embarrass anyone or hurt anyone. And he of course was utterly unchanged.

"Are you saying there's something wrong with him? What?"

"I don't know, Dana. He doesn't complain about anything, he isn't grouchy, he doesn't seem bored with me, and yet—there's something."

"A woman. What else could it be? If he has no problems at his job, if he's not sick, it's the only plausible explanation. Excuse me for blurting this out with such cruelty, Doina, but I can't imagine what else."

"No, I don't believe it's that. I should feel it. It's not that."

"Then what?"

"I don't know. I can't reproach him about anything."

"Well, just let it run its course."

"That's what I'm doing, Dana. That's what I'm doing."

Autumn came, and Michael moved back from Doina's parents' to their apartment. School began. In the evenings they stayed home with him to help him with his letters. A child makes life steadier and more serene, right? Puts the cement on a marriage, keeps your feet on the ground.

"What did you do today in school, little man?"

"Little *b* by hand, Daddy. Look at it, look at it, how fat the little *b* is, what a tummy it has."

"And anything else?"

"Well, the drawing lesson."

"Let me see what you did in drawing."

"A train, Daddy! Look at the train I drew."

"All the children had to draw a train?"

"No, Daddy. Anything that we wanted. Only it had to go. Some made tractors, others bicycles. One of them made a turtle, but that's not out of iron so it wasn't good. The lady explained that to him. I made a train. See!"

Liviu held him by his frail shoulders and stared deep into his son's eyes as if he wanted to find something there in the clear blue. For the first time before this small being who never before had seemed to resemble him, he felt a helplessness, a tenderness, a boundless pity.

"Michael, are you happy?"

The child made his eyes big with wonder and blinked.

"Happy? What do you mean, Daddy? What's that?"

■ □ ■ □ ■

THE TELEPHONE

THEY WAITED MORE THAN A QUARTER OF AN HOUR FOR THE BUS, which didn't come. It was Saturday evening, and they had no other alternative than to walk. So without a word they decided to cut through the group of apartment buildings, and likewise without a word they walked along the almost deserted streets, over which the summer sky with all its stars had settled democratically.

"Let's get a move on. You know they're waiting and can't start canasta without us." The man's voice showed no hint of anger or hurry or boredom. In that same tonality it could have addressed the interchangeable concrete apartment buildings, the asphalt still soft from the day's heat, the trees, the garbage cans lining the edge of the sidewalk. Except that *she* is walking beside him, in her best dress, the white one with little black flowers, and trying, as she did so often, not to think of anything. She knows that she will have to smile to the two or three acquaintances *from there* and that she will smile the same way to the others, the new faces he will introduce her to: my wife. She will pretend that she doesn't understand the meaningful glances, the furtively exchanged looks combining curiosity and a wry touch of wonder, perhaps pity as well. No, not pity. Amusement, rather. The idea of occasionally taking your legal wife to a group of friends who all know . . . It makes them hesitate a few seconds between embarrassment and excessive volubility, seconds that always torture her, fill her with nausea and helpless fury. But she has no choice, and about once a month she goes with him on this visit, knowing for more than two years how things stand, and knowing, too, that they know she knows. And above all knowing what he's thinking about at this moment, walking beside her in silence. Whom he's thinking about, more precisely. While she her-self is thinking about home or, more accurately, that apartment of theirs improperly called home, where there are two sleeping school-age children, an electric bill on top of the television set, and to-mato soup, rice pilaf, and some butter for Monday's school sand-wiches in the refrigerator.

Each time she goes there on Saturdays, along the way she remem-bers that phone call last summer which she hadn't the strength to wait for, the unseemly haste with which she left the apartment half an hour before. Maybe that man never called her, and then . . . she says to herself . . . then what? You're a fool, Gina told her, a mess. Your husband comes home as if it's a hotel, no, a boardinghouse, that's the better word to describe it. And you? What are you waiting for? For Prince Charming to come and make emergency repairs on you . . . by what, by force? Look, no prince is going to show up. Especially if you're so easily frightened off, so damn flighty.

But that man, if he really wanted to find her, he'd have searched for her the next day and the day after, too, right? If he really wanted her. What are you talking about? said Gina. There are oceans of women, baby! Who's got the time and the temperament, the sheer patience to pick up women for therapeutic purposes, to cure them of their complexes and their loneliness, the darkness that comes after the age of thirty-five when the legal husband is surveying the fiery contingent of twenty-to-twenty-five-year-old mares, all in heat? And this was the Gina who once told her how from ten in the morning until twelve midnight she waited for a phone call, startled by every ring, crying and laughing while furiously cleaning the wardrobe and tearing *his* photos to little pieces. Hers, too. And flinging the tele-phone to the floor and finishing that unforgettable day in despair by devouring everything she could find in the refrigerator.

And I'll tell you something incredible—you won't believe this, Gina had added. About a month after that sordid episode, I read a short story in some provincial magazine or other, a story by an American, Margaret I-don't-know-what, and right there—amazing!—in black and white, with all the gory details, she told my unhappy story with the telephone. Let me tell you, it was just the same—what I did, even what I thought, all of it, minus only the grand finale with the eating. So I said to myself, Baby, nothing's ever new. Our reactions are standard, the events computerizable, and no matter the parallel or meridian, we're all of us incalculably stupid.

What is Gina doing now, this very Saturday night on which, she knows, after five more blocks, she'll arrive where she has to smile and be polite?

Gina must have gone with somebody in his car to a mountain resort, maybe Sinaia or Predeal—or she's home alone, and on Monday she'll say she was at Predeal or Sinaia.

Now they're about to turn right after passing the wall covered by wisteria. She knows the route with her eyes closed. And in fact she does close them. Then stops. From a first-floor apartment across the street, a telephone can be heard ringing, its shrill sound piercing the soft, warm quiet of this deserted street in this lifeless corner of the world. The telephone goes on ringing insistently, ringing and ringing without stop. And in that apartment there's nobody. Suddenly she feels that she can't endure it anymore, that her eyes are about to fill with tears. She knows, yes, it's madness, utter folly, but she'd like to run, break down the door, enter that strange house, and now, now, now, pick up the receiver. She knows she's not the one this long, desperate ringing is addressed to, she knows she's not the one being sought. She knows that nobody is searching for her. She stands dumbly, crushing her bag between her hands while the man waits, smoking, ten paces ahead, and the telephone goes on ringing and ringing ceaselessly, ever farther away, ever more quietly, in a strange house where there's nobody at all.

LOCAL NEWS

HE ENTERED IN SLOW MOTION AND SHUT THE DOOR FIRMLY BEHIND him. Carefully, he slid a hand into his pocket where he had put the box of razor blades. There it was. For a few seconds his fingers rested on the smooth edge of the box. For such a business, surely it's better to have a brand-new blade. And he did. The fluorescent light above the sink flickered annoyingly. Without proceeding farther into the room, he let his gaze inspect the water-splotched walls, the faded curtain over the window, the damaged ceiling. Not even the mirror is the way it should be, he said to himself when, finally, he stood in front of it. Already he felt pains in his eyes. For more than two months, every time he entered the bathroom, he tried to remember where else he might have seen this flickering light, and he couldn't figure it out. (In some other bathroom, Father.) He raised his left hand to brush back his hair, a gesture from his youth; the movement froze in the air several times. Then suddenly he saw again the precise arc of the drummer's arm, the trajectory of the boy's arm dissected by the stroboscope. (Stroboscope, Father, that's what this device is called.) The concert hall in darkness, about one hundred young people, a scattering of parents who came to see their children, grown up into high school students, onstage. That performance had exhausted him and given him pains in his eyes. Now, too, his eyes pulsed in pain, with each flicker of the fluorescent tube accompanied by a small noise which amplified his feeling of discomfort.

At last he took a look at his face in the mirror. He hadn't time to focus on any surface of it, for example, that plane from the corner of his eye to his temple, before the light suddenly interrupted his scrutiny and the "information" was erased, making him start over again. He touched his mustache tentatively, but his fingers trembled in the palsied image in the mirror, jumping millimeter by millimeter from the left to the right, as in a cartoon. "I'm going to grow a mustache, too. By the time we're back home, it'll be like yours. I'm sure the outcome will be decided in a month or so." But it wasn't to be one month; it was two and a good many more before they were transported back to Moldavia on the train for the wounded. But to his friend Spiru, Spiru from the second division (Spiru, and what was the family name?), he'd grown only a scattering of anemic hairs, reddish yellow: "Shave them. What the hell! Don't you get it? They'll never become a real mustache."

The corners of his mouth stretched apart in a smile—jerking likewise in the reflected image in the mirror.

When he came out of the bathroom, his son had already returned from the institute and was removing some papers from his bag. Looking at the old man and not at first figuring out the change in him, he asked if he were sick.

"Why do you think I'm sick?"

"I don't know. You look pale."

"I'm not pale. I shaved off my mustache."

"How come you shaved your mustache?" his son asked, aware at last that the change came from the disappearance of his mustache. "Why now?"

"Why not now?"

The outdoor market at the Union Plaza, May 18, eleven A.M.

P.C. crept along, one step forward, another step—a segment of a huge millipede whose happy head was at the table with strawberries. What was he thinking about sandwiched between the fat housewife with a weight lifter's neck and the skinny, dried-mackerel-like woman who kept shifting her bulging plastic bags from one hand to another? Of nothing bad. In a household with three men, where any feminine influence was absent—his wife by death, his daughter-in-law by desertion—with a nephew at school, his boy at his job, who was supposed to take care of buying groceries if not he? But, no, he wouldn't complain. He was healthy, in full possession of his wits, he had seen a great deal in life and was able to accept almost everything. Well, well, this is my situation now, but it's not carved in stone, so let's live and we'll see. Let me stay healthy, that's the important thing, because if a man has his health, he can rise above any troubles.

He, too, heard loud cries, some woman's strident voice, but he didn't turn his head. If you're in a market, you're in a market. The woman's words got through to him only at the exact instant when the hands of the woman weight lifter grabbed him by the shoulders and the mackerel caught his wrists with fingers like sticks. Months afterward, despite himself, he was obliged to remember, often in the most unsuitable moments, the pressure on his hands of the mackerel's dark fingers, strong as if woven of cane. Then he saw the excited crowd turning its attention from the strawberries and rapidly forming an angry platoon of soldiers. They surrounded him and at the same time pushed him, pushed him. Where to?

One-forty-five P.M. A chilly room.

Characters: One woman around sixty-five years old. One policeman behind a desk. Two other policemen behind two smaller desks. He recognized the cries from the market. They belonged to that woman.

Tired voice: "What is it you say he took from you, and why?"

"All my savings, the beast, every last leu of my money. My life savings, from scrimping and saving my whole lifetime. He told me that he would arrange to get my car through customs, and I believed him because I saw he looked like a respectable old gentleman." She made a spitting noise at him. "Ptooey! Robber, thief, they should grind you to dust, mash you to a pulp!" Et cetera, et cetera.

Tired voice: "And where did this incident happen? And what is his name?"

"But how could I know his name? I'd know the name of this pickpocket, this swindler, this . . ." Et cetera, et cetera.

Tired voice: "How could you *not* know, woman, *not* know his name? Well, then, how can you be so sure this man is the perpetrator? On what basis do you recognize him?"

"It must be this one because I know it can't be anyone else, that's for sure, because I recognize him by his criminal look, by his mustache, and by his bunions. Take his shoes off and you'll see how big they are, because that one, the one who took my money, he had

bunions like this"—here the woman showed her bony red fist—
"and the one who took my hard-earned savings is this beggarly old
pig, this con man with his bunions like this. Off with your shoes,
good-for-nothing bastard, off with them, because otherwise *I'll* be
the one to, and *I'll* take them off with your shit-heel feet as well!" Et
cetera, et cetera.

As if on purpose, his laces slithered away through his fingers. They
seemed suddenly to be incredibly limp, slippery, flopping about or
wriggling like worms in his hands, which were awkward and lifeless
now when they should have been firm and strong—for God's sake,
he had nothing to hide! If this madwoman wants proof, she'll get her
proof, and let's put an end to this mess (no part of which could he
understand at all). He stayed bent over, working feverishly with the
laces, as all the blood rushed into his head, creating a darkness before
his eyes. His heart—*thump-thump* in his throat, *thump-thump*—the
hell with it. I didn't die at the Bend of the Don, and now she's killing
me, this raving old bag. He breathed deeply and finally took his left
shoe off. The old woman charged forward and yanked at his sweaty
sock, throwing him over one of the tables.

"This one doesn't have a thing. Let's see the other."

Just the same. Nothing.

Wonder and consternation, another deluge of curses. Nonethe-
less, disbelief—and her suspicion totally intact.

"Your full name?" asked the tired voice.

"Carnation Ciurelu . . . Harmony Street number —— . . . profession? . . . seven children! . . . that's my profession . . . seven!"

"Full name?" asked the voice again.

"P.C. . . . the Berceni district . . . street number —— . . . retired."

The policeman wrote another two lines, and then he said, "OK,
that's all. And *you*"—addressing the woman—"you'd better take care
of your memory because it's rather poor. Look, we've wasted time
over nothing, and the state doesn't pay us to waste time, understand? Got it? Well, shake hands, and you can go."

The market of the Union Plaza, May 18, five P.M.

No trace of strawberries. To give up so much time and come back
home empty-handed. He felt in his pocket to see if his plastic shopping bag were still there. It was. And his money? Let's see, in this

crazy mess, maybe he left without his hundred. No, there it is, a hundred-lei note—blue, carefully folded, unwrinkled, crisp and new, a hundred-lei note. Goood, he sighed to himself. Goood. Let's go home. Enough for one day.

And only when he decided to leave the market did he realize—and at first he didn't quite believe it, but the sensation was unmistakable—his toes freely reached the paper or plastic lining of his shoe, whatever it might have been made of, because he knew it couldn't have been leather. Well, oh my, even worse, oh my, so this is his situation—he was barefoot in his shoes. He had forgotten his socks there. Dear God, what a shame! The whole way to the trolley and the whole way on the trolley, he could think of nothing but his sweaty brown socks. And because he couldn't envision where the madwoman, that old hag, had thrown them, he imagined either that they had dropped on the desk with a lamp or that they were hanging over the middle officer's chair or on the picture frame; maybe they were somewhere among the policeman's papers, maybe they had kept on floating through the chill of the room. Oh, Lord, Lord, what a shame! Let me make it home to my own room quickly, not meet anyone who knows me. Most of all, let Radu not find out anything. Such matters are not to be spoken about. Especially after a certain age, and he was that age, it wasn't good to mention at home that an incident like this had happened to someone you knew, let alone to you.

"Oh, Mr. P.C.? From the third floor? Nice old man. Retired. I never noticed anything, and you know that I have such a civic sense of observation. . . . Why? Does he want to travel somewhere? Bulgaria? Maybe farther? No? Well. It's his business what he's done. His and yours, of course. He lives with his son, who is a kind of draftsman, and with his nephew, a high school student. His daughter-in-law ran away with another man three years ago. Oh yes, that girl, yes, she had roving eyes, that girl did, and she used to smoke, too. Well, I think you get the picture, don't you? The old man, come to think of it, I wonder about him, but before you asked, I never observed anything. He was even invited to my daughter's school as a war hero. They say a shell splinter—he was operated on in a hospital in Moldavia—he's got only half his stomach. Why he should need a full ration, I don't know, since he's got a smaller stomach, but well, if that's the way it was decided, for me these decisions might as well be holy, so it's not my problem, you know? I'd say myself that it would be right to take away half his ration, but anyhow, that's it. That's the way things are. But he, well, after all, he's a war hero, maybe it was considered better this way. What else can I say, since he's this hero? In the end it's always proved that you don't ever know what to believe in—today a hero, some day soon a street with the name Hero Street, then one fine day a new street sign with Petunia Street, formerly Hero Street. That's our situation, ours is a time that makes everything clear in the end. But from him, no, I never expected . . . Because, well, if it was about Mr. Arnăutescu from the fifth floor or the Ionescus from the other entrance—yeah, better believe me, you know. But Mr. P.C.? I don't know anymore what to believe about this world, upon my word, I don't know what to believe."

The Berceni district, June 4, ten A.M.
It's good he took his umbrella with him. This rain, it will help the corn, and if it rains next April, maybe we'll have some wheat. But at least it's going well for the corn.

P.C. walked slowly, avoiding the puddles. It wasn't far to the grocery, about five minutes, surely they would have received some chicken or bacon in this morning's deliveries. His nephew had to pass his baccalaureate exams to graduate from high school. The boy must gain strength; he's getting weak from nervousness. And then the college entrance exam, too, oh God, what a summer. Maybe the boy will do well. What will be, will be—because, no matter what, the army makes a man of anyone.

He didn't even have a chance to get out of the way. A shove from behind and someone snatched the umbrella. The two burly tough guys who pushed him were now handing his umbrella back and forth over his head, two guys of about twenty or so with their shirts unbuttoned down to their navels. One of them, a damp cigarette butt between his lips, followed his amazement with great satisfaction.

"What're you doing, old geezer? Going wading in puddles? Oh, so, so sorry. You lost your balance? Drink something too strong so early in the morning? Le'go of the umbrella, old man, don'tcha dare put a paw on it, leave it alone! The rain'll be good for your hair! Well, with so much money, you carry a pretty shoddy umbrella," and *crack!* the mustached man on the left side bent three ribs, "and you wear this miserable raincoat," suddenly grabbing hold of his collar. "How come, old codger, how come? With all the loot you took, you're parading about in these here cheap clothes. Well, you're good material for the loony bin, the devil's own special asylum! Stand still, stand still! Everyone can see you then, like a soaked scarecrow! We'll hear them laugh at a clown like you. OK, OK, now we're gonna take you where you have to go, to spill it all out, 'cause the cops in Berceni aren't gullible like those pansies in the Union Marketplace. They won' let you waltz away scot-free. And we're not stupid and weak like our aunt to let you escape with all that damn money hot in your pocket. Come on, march, march! And not a peep outta you, 'cause we don' got the time, old man."

All the way to the police station, he was obsessed by one question: Had he, or had he not, put on clean socks? One by one, gradually, he wriggled all his toes from left to right—no, the socks had no hole, but he couldn't remember if they were completely clean or if they were the same pair he'd worn yesterday. Now, what more could he do? Oh my, that's the situation, and anyhow, he couldn't change anything. But maybe they were fresh from this morning.

At the police station everything repeated itself up to a certain point in the proceedings. Do you know this comrade? How could we not! His name is P.C., and he lives here in Berceni. But wait! How, how could these two goons possibly know his name and where he lives? Of course, of course, how could he forget? From the first oral statement when he had to give his name, occupation, and address. Of course, that was it. It adds a new element, a concrete fact. Oh my God.

After about half an hour the victim of the swindle showed up. Red like fire, wheezing from hurry and agitation. The same rain of cursing, complaints, oaths.

"Hell swallow this old fart! If not for these two boys of my brother, I couldn't have caught him, and all my money from my lifetime of honest work would go to the devil." And again questions, how, in what kind of circumstances, why, who else was there? And again the old fury answered with abuse, execrations, accusations, but nothing specific, and this made the interrogation more difficult. The two hooligans kept seconding what she said. Of course they knew all about the money, of course she'd had it. And the same story: "Then I gave the money to this one, to get my car through customs, and he, this decrepit ruptured sack of bones, because you know, you see him with white hair and think he's respectable, an example for everyone, and instead of this, he's a thief, comrade, a crook, an impostor."

"But beside his name, surname, and profession," asked the policeman, already tired of this, "which he says that you found out from the last interrogation, what other specifics can you tell me? Where, when, and how, because it's not at all clear. And if he's not the man? How can you identify him? It could be someone else he resembles. There's no evidence."

And then the old woman (oh ho, how long P.C. had been waiting for this moment) put forth, exasperatedly, her crucial evidence: "He's the one, how it could not be him? I know him by his criminal look, by his mustache, and by his bunions. Because that one who took my money had huge bunions like this, and that one is this one, this doddering horse turd, I don't know why you feel such pity for him, why you don't put him on ice forever, to know that he's behind bars, so I'll get my money back, because it's mine from my honest work, because today, I see, no, there's no more true honesty, honesty's good for nothing, it's better to be a felon and a filcher like him, because look"—turning to address P.C.—"what are you doing with the whole lot of your honesty? But I'm not giving up, you'd better know that, I'll go all the way, all the way to the top. Off with your shoes, toothless old pig, take them off, show us your huge bunions and make plain to Mr. Officer who and what you really are, you filthy swindling horse's ass."

P.C. untied his shoelaces. He took his socks off—oh yes, thank the Lord, they were clean, clean. He felt a huge relief, a kind of thankfulness and a sense of well-being. The group rushed to look at his feet.

"It seems that here, here on the left, there could be something here, yes, yes, maybe."

"No!" The old woman remained consistent with her own belief. "That one had such huge bunions, this one hasn't, may he soon be

LOCAL NEWS

with the devil, the dotard, maybe he cut them off, but I can't see any sign of it. Be so kind, sir, as to bring the lamp here. Let's see if there's a scar."

But not even with the help of the lamp could anything be discerned.

And then everything ended as the previous time.

"Lady, you have to look for someone else because he isn't the man you want," the policemen concluded. "And you'd better leave this man alone because you won't have him taking his shoes and socks off in every police station in Bucharest. Do you understand me?"

And that was all.

The street was almost deserted. When he passed in front of the grocery, P.C. peered through the window. It had been closed for a long time. I'll come here tomorrow, early in the morning. He felt his knees and his arms trembling slightly. Perhaps because of the cold of the window he was pressing his forehead against. Yes, that must be why. Slowly he moved back from the window, the distance of one hand. At that distance, his face, his eyes, came into focus. What kind of look? What was it that woman meant? The look, hmm, maybe it would be better to go to an eye doctor. To wear a pair of glasses. Yes, surely he needed glasses. And the mustache . . . he'd worn this mustache since he was twenty. Ioana married him with this mustache. Anyhow, tomorrow, after standing in line for chicken, he'll go to an eye doctor for glasses. How much could a pair of glasses for distance vision cost? Must be the same as for reading glasses. Yes, but he bought those twenty years ago, and the money was different then. Fifty, one hundred lei, let them cost however much they cost.

It wasn't the money he felt sorry about but the lost time, that and the outcome. Money, he would manage it somehow because Alecu would lend him some from his pension. At least the expense wouldn't be noticed at home.

Hadn't Alecu been the one who advised him to sue the old woman in court and request compensation? Because he was a man who'd fought in the war and almost left his bones there—should he be subjected to shame by a crazy old witch?

"What's that, old boy?" wondered Alecu after the trial. "So they said that you're a pair of old people, and lots of times it happens that the elderly become confused about things because the memory, the mind, the one, the other. So they can't take a thing like this seriously, because of the age of the two parties? You have to pay them? But why are you the one who has to pay for this? How can this be, old friend?"

"How come, old boy? Expenses for the trial, because they gathered together, they spent time, and time is money. That's how come."

The doctor told him he didn't need glasses for distance vision. Why should he want to get glasses if he sees very well? And he can still see very well.

He came home nervous. Hmm, his second pack of cigarettes today. Maybe he needed sleeping pills because three or four hours of fitful sleep each night wasn't enough.

He stared for a long time at his wedding picture. That's how it is, Ioana. Tomorrow I'm going to have a picture made. With my mustache. Then I'll be ready. I'll shave it.

Unexpectedly, he fell asleep very quickly. This hadn't happened to him the whole of the previous month.

He went out to shop less and less often. He didn't feel like leaving the apartment. Sorin passed his exams, so Radu gave him money for a vacation at the seaside. Good, very good, because the boy has tortured himself enough with memorizing books.

Now he was alone with Radu. At first, he felt some mild tingling in his foot, and then real pain.

"Is something wrong with you, Father? Aren't you feeling well? You seem sick, or else I'm not yet used to seeing you without a mustache."

Realizing that the pains were not decreasing but rather, in the last two weeks, they had grown stronger and stronger, he finally told Radu.

"You see, Father, you see, you're smoking too much. One day, God forbid, they'll have to cut your leg off, just like Uncle Dan, who smoked until he got arthritis. For God's sake, can't you keep

LOCAL NEWS

21

▼

from smoking so much? What kind of a sorrow is eating you up, what kind of troubles? What's the matter? You smoke one cigarette after another!"

Beginning the next day, he limited his smoking to only five cigarettes. Then to one after every meal. He seemed to start to feel better. Anyhow, if the evil came from forty years of smoking, the good couldn't come in a month. Autumn arrived with its rains. Maybe it could be from the weather, too. Although he hadn't smoked for three months, he could barely walk. He felt arrows shooting upward and into his hips.

"See, Father? You gave up smoking, and now you're better."

How could he tell him, No, son, it hurts like a wound, from head to toe?

If he looked at himself in the mirror—and since the day he shaved his mustache, he didn't feel much like looking in the mirror—he almost couldn't recognize himself. His eyes were clouded, watery. Since he had begun to have such terrible pains in his feet, he'd acquired another look. Of suffering held in, so his boy wouldn't find out. And no traces of a mustache, either. He took care of that daily. Yes, he almost couldn't recognize himself. That's good. That's very good. But the pains . . .

It could be the time has come—couldn't it? he said to himself. Anyhow, I ought to buy a new suit, a white shirt, and a pair of new shoes. Let me have them at hand. Better to be ready.

Outside the weather was almost balmy. From time to time in October, Bucharest turns unexpectedly warm. He decided to go out.

In the shoe store there were very few customers. He asked for a pair, size eight and a half. His shoe size for a lifetime. "The brown ones, or the black?" asked the salesperson—a young lady, with a clear gaze (whom did she resemble? she resembled someone dear, but he couldn't remember right away). Those black eyes. The girl returned with the shoes, and slowly he took off his own, and also slowly, he tried to put the left shoe on. He couldn't do it. He looked for a more comfortable position, tried again, but it was useless. Then the girl offered to help him. She kneeled, took the shoe with both hands, and began to bring it to the old man's foot, but her movement froze halfway. The girl raised her eyes (where had he seen those eyes? a long time ago? but where?), and she said quietly, as if she were ashamed, "You need another size, a bigger one at least or, better, another type of shoe that's more suitable for your problem. You know, we learned at shoe school that this model's never good for bunions like the ones you have."

■ □ ■ □ ■

THE FALLEN CORK TREE

WHAT GOOD WOULD IT DO HIM TO WEAR A WATCH? THE MINUTES never mattered, or even the hours. At eight every morning, the woman would come with the newspapers, and he skimmed them until eight-thirty, when Cristina would call. To check up on him? No, just routine: How are you? . . . reading the papers . . . anything new with you? . . . hell with that, and you? . . . with the girls at coffee . . . well, later today? . . . no, don't think so . . . OK . . . bye. Then he poured two coffees and when the Statistician made his appearance, he knew it was exactly a quarter to nine. At nine sharp, after they'd had their coffee, the Statistician left for his office, and he took out the current files, sorted them, and began to work. He worked for a while—how long? it didn't matter—and then let his mind drift as he wondered about all kinds of things. His little office, a former closet for office supplies, was the most intimate nook in the stark and massive building which was their workplace. He was happy to be alone. Nobody was there to peer over his shoulder. At twelve-thirty on Mondays and Fridays, the manager's secretary called him to request that he bring the current files. At one on Tuesdays, they called him to go the ministry building. On Thursdays, it was something else—he went out to see clients. So what good would it do him to wear a watch? What do you mean, what good? the Statistician would ask at the beginning. What kind of lawyer are you without a watch? I couldn't breathe even for a second without a watch, old man. I sleep with my watch on. And when I wash and I have to take it off, I feel, oh, I don't know, I feel embarrassed. I don't need it, the Lawyer responded. Wearing one makes me nervous. And if I need to I can go out into the corridor and check what time it is because, thank God, they have a clock on every floor—it's true that the hours are different from level to level, ha-ha—and if I don't feel like venturing out of my cave, I can dial the time-of-day number to find out, right? The Lawyer imitated, "At the tone the time is exactly eleven-twenty-three and ten seconds." So what does it matter! As he said this, the Lawyer would see in the Statistician's expression amazement coupled with an utter lack of understanding—nothing else. It would serve no purpose for him to explain why he gave up wearing a watch, a Longines his father had given him at the hospital before . . . The watch and the suspicious, uptight, conformist temperament inherited from his father.

Then he had looked at his watch every two minutes because *she* didn't call, *she* didn't come, where was *she* now? A childish thing. Yes, but it became a tic. The forearm twisting upward, the arm thrusting forward to free the watch face from his shirtsleeve. Not only the other students but also his constitutional law professor noticed it. It was at that point he had decided to take off his watch and leave it forgotten in a wardrobe, under his shirts. Where it still is. With Cristina everything was serene and easygoing. It was better that way. But probably the Statistician was right, too, whenever he preached his exasperating theory about predictability, planning, and all their advantages. No, the Lawyer and the Statistician weren't bosom buddies. They never could have been. They were friends for coffee breaks, for sports talk—no more than that.

From the first days when they had coffee together, the Statistician would expound upon his program for life: "Old man, I've got no worries, I'm at peace. I have an apartment, I'll get married, then I'll move to a bigger one, I'll have children, I'll buy a car, a VCR, a refrigerator, and other trifles, I'll grow a beer belly and turn bald. And that's just about it. Planning will do the trick. I know everything, step by step." He said this with such satisfaction, so voluptuously, although this word, *voluptuously*, could hardly have been associated with the Statistician.

"There's no coefficient of risk, of unpredictability?"

"None, old man. Absolutely out of the question. Everything depends on me only. Not because I'm chief devil in this world, Old Scratch himself, but because these are standard outcomes which cannot be realized at less than one hundred percent probability. I don't even seek other things because I know what's to happen to me can turn out only as I want it to happen. That's why I make it my custom to want usual, controllable, sure things to happen to me."

"But if . . ."

"There's no *if* in my program, old man, which, you see, is a very simple one. My plans are the simplest, in fact. House, wife, children, a few possessions. And all this dependent on me. Contingency comes into play only when something doesn't depend on you, those random occasions when you see ghosts or a blue moon. So as not to suffer from insomnia, frustration, and disappointment, I've decided to wish for what I know I can have, come what may. Get it?"

The Lawyer could have contradicted him. And how! But he didn't. In truth he felt it's good that in this world there are some naive souls like this man, people who believe that they can protect themselves from indeterminacy, exclude chance from their calculations. And until now the Statistician had calculated well. With just a minor deviation in chronology. He indeed got a small apartment, but his second step wasn't marriage—instead, the purchase of a car. Well, it doesn't matter, this isn't a deviation from the plan but an inconsequential readjustment of its stages. Oh yeah!

Then why the hell has he been drinking coffee with him for more than three years when the Statistician's infantile confidence is already such a bore? Maybe because it makes him feel good to see someone devoid of fear of the unpredictable? Or maybe coffee on the dot of eight-forty-five was part of the Statistician's compulsory plan, and he, willingly or unwillingly, had become part of this plan? How would it be if some morning he simply greets him, No, today, let's not drink coffee, or, I want to have mine later, at ten? Ha! Turn him topsy-turvy, spoil his little game, bring him back to earth smack on his feet! Because, paradox of paradoxes, the Statistician, the inflamed zealot of planning, the partisan of predictability, is really the one more up in the clouds, more fantastical, if he thinks that life is, oh yeah . . . could be . . . the hell with it!

He had thought about this scenario several times previously, with a kind of malicious joy, and was on the point of acting on it, but, who knows why, he gave it up at the last second. Let him be. It's his business. So when the Statistician came in, the Lawyer invariably said, Hi, here it is, coffee's ready, and the expression on the

Statistician's face seemed to say, Of course, how else might it be? And in the ensuing quarter of an hour the usual banal conversation, sports scores, harmless, petty gossip about the soccer league where the Statistician had a cousin. When the Lawyer found out that the Statistician was an avid hunter, of all things, he was a little bit perplexed. A hunter? Like some gentrified sportsman or landed aristocrat of the old days? No, he couldn't suspect him of being snobbish. And the idea that the Statistician could do it out of passion, I mean that this man could do anything out of passion, seemed to him terribly implausible.

"Come on, my friend, to be a skilled hunter and never breathe a word about it, just a tiny hint, or some hunting anecdote, at least. To leave us with no more that the latest sports achievements to talk about. Don't keep it to yourself!" The Statistician looked at him in wonder: What kind of stories, man? All that stuff is . . . is fanciful, silly invention. What could happen during a hunt? You get ready and you hunt. I go for the purpose of practicing my precision, that's what I'm doing. I'm giving my precision its exercise. That's why I hunt. You aim at your target, you hit it. Nothing more.

The Lawyer tried once or twice again to ask, Hey, how did the hunting go? But each time the Statistician answered him brusquely, How could it go? You aim at your target, you hit it. So by now he'd given up raising the topic.

That's why he won't ask him today, although he knows that yesterday the Statistician went where he usually goes—to the pond for a duck shoot. Outside it's raining in torrents, you almost cannot see beyond the window. Autumn is here. Dampness and darkness. The Lawyer stands to switch on the light, and at that moment his hand accidentally brushes against the cup. The liquid splashes violently. It isn't this that upsets him, however, but the fact that his fingertips have touched a smooth, cold surface, the cold of the cup. How can that be? He sits back down on the chair and holds the two cups in his palms. They are cold. It means that . . . No, it can't be. Cristina had called him at eight-thirty, and after that he had immediately started the coffee. And then? He stands up and goes out into the corridor: nine-thirty. He can't believe his eyes. Is it really nine-thirty? Why doesn't he dial the time-of-day number? Is he afraid of precision, does he prefer the dubious clock in the corridor? Come on, man, let's be serious, he says to himself, furious at his own reaction, and with an overexaggerated, deliberate energy, he dials for the time: ". . . is exactly nine-forty-two and twenty seconds. *Clink!* At the tone the time is exactly nine-forty-two and thirty seconds. *Clink!* At the tone the time is . . ." What? What could have happened to this fellow nothing ever happens to? Do you miss him somehow? No, but . . . but what? It just can't be. You've gone crazy, too, haven't you? Why can't something unexpected happen even to him? Maybe he has a toothache, maybe some relative from the country arrived, anything could happen. Even to him? Damn it, yes. You've caught a case of his craziness, that's it. You're addlebrained, you're suggestible and mindless. A jackass, that's what you're being.

"Hi." In the frame of the open door, the massive silhouette of the Statistician. "Am I disturbing you? Are you working?"

"No. Come in, come in. Wait a second until I reheat this slop."

The Statistician sits and looks out the window. "Sure is raining like hell." This is the first time the Lawyer has ever seen him gaze absently out the window and likewise the first time he's heard him commenting on what he sees.

"You turned on the light."

"Yeah. It was so dark here."

"Of course. We shouldn't ruin our eyes, should we? So turn it on, that's the right thing. Down there, down in the underground, it'll be dark. So dark."

A sentence like this must be an absolute novelty in the Statistician's inventory of thoughts.

Perhaps he has a fever, perhaps his stomach's upset, perhaps—and the Lawyer doesn't dare to say the simplest thing in the world—perhaps something's happened to him.

He's embarrassed and confused, the Lawyer; he spills half the coffee into the saucer and tries to calm himself down by telling himself that no doubt he's being utterly ridiculous. This must be one of the most commonplace scenes possible between two fellow workers in any firm, the most banal kind of daily dialogue, there's nothing unusual about it. What the hell, his nerves are frazzled, that's the one clear thing. While he's thinking this, or trying to think it, the Statistician, staring at the rivulets of rain running down the windowpanes, says to him, "Let me tell you something." Then pauses.

Now, of course . . . he's sure that now the Statistician is going to tell him, as usual, who married whom, which player was sold or which goalie was bought by another team, or—the Lawyer feels himself calming down, everything's turning normal again, the banal, the customary, the ordinary that has bored and exasperated him for three years.

"Yesterday I went hunting."

The Lawyer's voice can barely be heard over the rain. "Yes, I know."

"What? How? How do you know?" The Statistician fixes him with his eyes, which the Lawyer seems to notice for the very first time. Black, deep black.

"From you, of course. How else could I have known? Didn't you tell me that on Saturday you were to go to the pond after ducks?"

"Oh yes . . . well . . ."

This pause is deeply irritating to the Lawyer. He is eager to be told at once what this fellow has to tell him because, finally, it's clear to him that the Statistician's got something to tell. But the Lawyer knows he shouldn't push him. Let him speak when he feels like it. He'll want to because he wouldn't have started otherwise, and he might say only, You aim at your target, you hit it.

"This whole business, it's quite something . . . it's something, something else," the Statistician tries to begin again after a while. "There . . . I mean I have no idea what the hell's going on because . . ." And then he turns and remains silent with his black eyes staring out the window.

"Hey, take a second and gather your thoughts, man," the Lawyer can't help saying. "Then try to tell me what it is, for God's sake, because I assume that something's happened, hasn't it?"

"Hmm, yeah. It happened. Something. I mean, I don't know, I can't make clear sense of anything, that's it, I don't feel any certainty at all. Yet I have the proof. The proof. Well, maybe you'll understand better than me because I can't—because, I mean, it's something that I can't . . . OK, I'll tell you everything, and you tell me what you think about the whole business. All right?"

"Get on with it, old man! Is it something so awful?"

"No, no. But I still can't make sense of it, how it . . . Well, we'll see in the end. Anyway, I went to the same place I've been going for more than two years, and I wanted to stay overnight at the Village Watchman's as usual, where I've stayed since the very first times I went hunting and where I feel so comfortable because I like the bed and the small room, and in the mornings we would go together . . . Well, I'm on my way to his place when he lets me know he's sorry, this time I can't stay the night, some relatives of his from Transylvania have come unexpectedly—you hear? unexpectedly—so I would have to stay overnight with the Forest Ranger. And he's sure it's nice enough there, too, he's arranged everything, and he hopes I'm not going to be upset, he had no choice, he's sorry, that's the way it's got to be. Something absolutely unforeseen with those cousins from Transylvania, cousins or whatever the hell they might be. I became uneasy but I had no other choice. I didn't like this surprise at all, do you understand? Not at all."

"A triviality, such nonsense! So what if you didn't get to sleep where you usually do? What's the big deal? In my opinion, a man who calls himself a hunter must be able to sleep anywhere, under the open sky, too."

"Well, of course, I know those things myself, but you see, I'd grown very used to staying at the Village Watchman's, and this unforeseen thing made me so nervous, I can't tell you how upset. Do you understand?"

"No, I don't."

"Damn it, have it your way. No use explaining to you! I had a habit and now . . . Oh, the hell with it. I went there, to the Ranger's, way at the edge of the village, the last house. And I didn't like the guy. From the very moment I saw him, I didn't like him. And you've known me long enough to know I don't have prejudices. In fact, the way he ordered *her* to bring this thing or that thing, the fact that he sat there puffing his cigarette like a helpless invalid while *she* lugged the heavy water buckets, and . . ."

"*She?* What *she?*" The Lawyer is hesitant to interrupt.

The Statistician raises his demitasse of coffee and slowly takes a sip—probably nothing in the cup but cold, gritty dregs that have settled to the bottom.

"The woman. That woman. A young woman. His wife, I presume. His woman. I don't know because he didn't introduce her and she was always silent. He kept her scurrying from here to there, wherever he asked her to go: Take the sheets, put them in the big room, cook some potatoes, fetch some meat from the larder. Just like that, from here to there, one place to another. And she dared to look up with her green eyes only when waiting for him to give orders."

"So what? That's the countryside. Women never escape from under men's words. What's the big deal? Is that all? This is what's thrown you for a loop? Really? Or, oh ho! Hadn't you better admit at once that it was love at first sight for this green-eyed country wench?"

"Come on, man, with your stupid ideas, it's not as simple as it seems because after that . . ." The Statistician pauses once again.

The Lawyer would like to tease him a little, to say, Bravo, my friend, an idyll in nature with an undomesticated rural creature who holds her tongue but earns an A plus plus. You don't deserve anything like this, you dumb-ass jerk, with all your absurd planning. But he says none of these things aloud because he wants to let him relate the whole story his own way.

"Listen to me," the Statistician says to gain time.

"I'm listening. Can't you see I am?"

"Yeah, I see. OK, I went to bed and, worst of all, I couldn't fall asleep. And after a while"—again a pause—"after a while, she came." Pause. "The woman. That woman. Just like that, without a word, she stood stiffly near my bed in the dark of midnight, I hadn't the slightest idea whether this was reality or merely a dream, and now I still don't know, I swear I don't know, because why should a crazy thing like this happen to me? Why? Tell me why! With one hand she lifted the blanket from me, and with the other she removed her scarf from her head. Then I saw, or it seemed to me that I saw, a red flame, her hair was a red flame, and under that flame I saw a pathway. She led me from bed, from that room, drew me somewhere to a field of mint, and there, in that field of mint, old man, it seemed the whole earth split in two, that's how it was, that's how it seemed to be. I've never felt such a thing in my life, with any woman, do you understand me? And I saw her hair like a flame in the sky, up and down, up and down, my God, she was pulsing up and down, and with both hands she clutched the mint and then let it fall. I suppose I myself grabbed some small sprigs of mint in my hands to reassure myself I was still alive. I don't know, either, when I got back or how. Early in the morning the Forest Ranger came and woke me, and I was in the same bed in the same room. When I went to wash up, I saw her, but I couldn't understand anything anymore. She didn't give me the least glance. She didn't utter a word. It was as if nothing, nothing had happened at all. She had a scarf very tight around her head, and I couldn't even see if she had fox-colored hair that flamed like I just told you. Not a glance, not the smallest sign. Nothing. So I said to myself, Well, it's clear, everything was in my mind, only in my mind. But why, man, why should I have hallucinations like this? I'm a very down-to-earth man, completely well adjusted. At the pond I missed every shot. It was the first time I failed totally. Then, on the way back, I decided to go, what the hell, to go see a psychiatrist, to see about all this." And the Statistician stops again.

"Go see one if you like. But don't take it all tragically because this is the sort of problem that happens to people frequently enough."

"Not to me, old man, not to *me*. I . . ."

"You're naive—excuse me, I should have told you a long time ago. You're very naive. An innocent who believes life can be computerized. Look, it can't. Forget it. Let it be. Take a vacation or some Valium, that's my advice. Or, if you'd rather, see a shrink. But if we feel we need a shrink to talk about all the things that escape our control, every one of us would need to go all the time. And it wasn't a nightmare. No, the opposite. It really was a pretty pleasant dream, wasn't it?"

"I'm not going to a psychiatrist. What could a shrink tell me? But on Saturday I'm going back there. I have to. Understand? I have to. Because . . . Look—look what I found yesterday evening in my pocket." The Statistician digs his hand into his pocket and holds out a fistful of mint.

On the third floor, the clock reads ten-twenty, on the fourth, ten-forty-five, and on the fifth, ten-fifty.

Just imagine the surprise of the Village Watchman when he sees me, because he thinks I'm returning to hunt three weeks from now. Would they have left, those cousins of his, whatever they are? Maybe they're gone. Whether they are or not, I'm going to look around the Ranger's again to see if . . . again . . . That's too much, isn't it? What? What do I think I'll find? But then why have I come here, why did I take the train and this awful bus, because it's not for the sake of ducks I'm here now. Let's be serious. I must clear up this business. If the mint hadn't been there, I would have said, like the Lawyer, it's an invention of my subconscious or else of the devil. But I have proof in my pocket. Proof. The hell with you and these dreadful roads and this dust! What? Excuse me. No, miss, I don't know where you have to get off for Cireşani, I'm going to another village. Ask the driver. She must be a new teacher, that's what she must be, poor, unfortunate girl, assigned to teach children in this godforsaken place. No, I'm not from here, I don't know. Talk to the mayor, he'll give you directions. What a long nose she has, nails like a corpse's, imagine those nails! Let her enjoy her idea of elegance now because in a very short time she won't have them at all after she has to go work with the schoolchildren harvesting potatoes. Yes, I'm getting off here, good day. What would have been in her mind? And those cousins from Transylvania, what were they looking for here? Why on earth did they have to spoil my routine? Maybe they've left. Oh no, no, on the contrary, one of them is over there, that fat guy with a mustache polishing his Skoda. And the Watchman, Mr. Sache, how proud he must be to have such well-off relatives who own a car come to visit him. Hello there, Uncle Sache. Well, no, no particular reason, I just felt like hunting. What? Aren't you going to the pond tomorrow? You see, I knew it! Oh, I understand, Uncle Sache, I understand, no problem, I'll go to the Forest Ranger's. What else can I do? That's the situation. No, no problem at all, but kindly send your little Vasile to let him know I'll be coming. First, Uncle Sache, your good homemade plum brandy—shall we drink a glass of your ţuică together? Oh, of course, you're right, I didn't used to drink, I didn't. Now, though, I just feel I should, and by God, I'll definitely have a ţuică.

"Kindly drink one more cup with me, Mr. Lawyer. Look at how it steams. This draws out every last bit of the cold. Your friend, too, then, before, you know, on the previous evening, when he arrived and asked me for a *ţuică*, the first time in those three years, and I was so astonished because you know he never used to drink, and suddenly, then, twice he drank a *ţuică*, twice. And he said that after

THE FALLEN CORK TREE

33
▾

we finished going after ducks he'd like to come back here like all the others always did, to stop by here, I mean, and drink another. I said to myself, well, something in him has changed, so I said to myself and so I thought, ignorant man that I am, so I thought. Right away I thought that the man is changing because of some great happiness or, who knows?—a misfortune. But I said to myself that a misfortune it couldn't have been, and I said again it must be a joy, and, excuse me, sir, for what better kind of joy could there be for a man than a woman, beg your pardon, sir, because, I must speak the truth, woman is bliss, no matter that there are some who say that woman's a great trouble, because I"—this with a lowered voice and a glance behind him toward the kitchen where his wife was busy—"I've had only happiness from women, this is God's truth, you have to know it. And I said in my ignorant mind, look, the gentleman is about to marry or is planning to be married and this future woman of his, what a shame, she won't let him hunt. When my little Vasile came back from the Ranger and told him that he could go there, he left. He simply stood up and left immediately. But please, have another, Mr. Lawyer, because when it cools, it's not so good. Now it's drawing out every last bit of the cold from deep in your bones."

So pour another small one, Uncle Sache, ah, to a new life. Fine, early tomorrow morning at five at the signalman's hut. Who else is coming along? The executive director of the warehouse for . . . and the actor? Oh, look at us, sir, only the best society! And after hunting, shall we gather here together? Well, Uncle Sache, you are right, man is always changing. I know that, after hunting, you used to ask me to come have a glass with the others. I don't know why I was in such a hurry to catch the first bus and the first train as if children were crying for me at home. What a dunce I used to be! But now, now after shooting those beauties, we'll come by here, and . . . Well, Uncle Sache, until tomorrow, five, near the signal.

A new life. Why shouldn't alcohol, in moderation, have its own purpose, too, why not? Must be ahead, there, at that light. The far edge of the village. Why doesn't this lazy Ranger repair his gate? Maybe he waits for her to do it, to do it all, she does it all. Good evening. No, I didn't think I'd be coming back so quickly, either, when I told you that. No, thank you, I'm not hungry. Well, if she made it, I'll take two, only two of them. What stars, Mr. Ranger, what glorious stars. Tomorrow will be clear, very clear. Enough conversation, this guy, anyhow, makes you nervous. But she, where is she now? At a neighbor's, somewhere in the village, at the store, because this guy, not even dead would he be moved from his front porch. Here she is, here, with the bedding in her arms, preparing the bed. In the same dark dress, with the same scarf around her head. Good evening. Strange, she scarcely nodded her head. And she looked at you furtively with those green eyes of hers. Why does she avoid gazing straight into your eyes? What does she want, this woman? Nothing from you, imbecile, it was a hallucination of yours. Don't you see that she doesn't take any notice of you? She isn't pleased and she isn't amazed. No, it's as if she knew you'd come, the sly fox! Thank you, Mr. Ranger, I don't believe I want to sit here any later. Tomorrow I have to be up early. I have to meet Mr. Sache at the signal house at five. Good night. Well, we'll see how good this night will be. Now I'll clear up this business for myself. They've made a fire, this early in the year they make fires. Of course, if he's a ranger, no problem getting the wood, of course. The flames in the fireplace, like her hair against the sky then, up and down, up and . . .

What? What is it? It's four already? Thank you, Mr. Ranger, huh, once I used to wake up on my own, and now . . . No, I won't eat anything before hunting, don't you recall from the last time? Yes, a glass of milk, yes. That'll be all. I'll wash and then I'll go. Well, so it's that way. Really, nothing. That's the way it is. I think I must have dreamed it, then. And the mint? The devil knows, it could be I took her without realizing it, that's clear to me. Oh mother, brrr, the water's so icy it hurts. Where did I put my shirt? I keep turning round and round like a top. Where? Why can't I find it? Look at her on the veranda. She's standing the way she did last time, near the bed, so stiffly. She's staring at me, staring with those green eyes. What a jerk I am, not even able to say good morning, something, anything. Why can't I say anything? In her arms, what's that? My God, it's my rifle, with the stock on the ground. Her hands, they're sliding up and down along the barrel! What the devil is she doing with it now, with my rifle? Why? The barrel's under her breasts. Put the rifle down! If you value your life, you mustn't ever keep a rifle like that with the barrel up because you never know. Put the rifle down! She's laughing, she's saying

something—what?—what's she repeating, repeating? Today I'm com-
ing with you, I'm coming with you, today I'm coming there. Oh, it isn't
possible that she could say, let alone mean, such a thing, I must be
imagining things again, and this woman, she's . . . But, oh my God,
along her temple, what's that right there? A stream of blood, oh Lord,
a stream of blood! You fool, you stupid idiot, it's a wet curl of her hair
escaped from that black scarf of hers, that's all. A curl of her red hair.
It's good, the milk, it's very good. And now I'll be leaving. Good health
to you. My hunting rifle, my gear, all ready, must move on quickly, it's
a quarter to five and Mr. Sache is waiting. And . . . did she say she'd
be coming? Did she really say such a thing? Come where? There? Why?
It's patently obvious that I must have hallucinated. It only seemed she
was saying she'd be coming, you idiot, it's more than certain you're ill,
mentally ill, crazy. So Monday I'll go to the doctor if . . . Could she be
behind me? Could she follow by another route? How can she know our
place? I'm not going to turn my head. I won't. No. No. No. Certainly
on Monday . . .

Good morning, Uncle Sache. Long life, Mr. Director, the honor is
mine. And you, sir, what play are you are rehearsing these days? Oh,
great, great. Nothing new in our field. Figures, plans, routine audits,
reports. Nothing more. Yes, excellent weather. We're lucky. The same
team, yes, yes indeed. As usual, I'll take the right, I'll be the one farthest
to the right. In my customary spot, there at the fallen cork tree.

"And there, what took place there?"

"Where, Mr. Lawyer?"

"At the pond?"

"As I already told you. We each went to our places. His was farthest to the right, at the fallen cork tree. It was the spot he always
took. If you could stay until tomorrow, I'd show you, we could go,
it's not all that far."

"No, Uncle Sache, I can't stay until tomorrow."

"I understand, Mr. Lawyer. Although I'm a simple man, I understand. Job, business. I know from my older son."

"And?"

"And what? Oh, the ducks flew past, we took aim and shot them,
and then . . ."

I think I've turned fat, otherwise all these things wouldn't seem so heavy. I wouldn't be panting like this, my heart wouldn't be pounding. OK, I have to see a cardiologist, too. On Monday. Well, at least the cork tree is in its right place. But where did you think it might be, you moron? Where else? Oh hell, now you're wondering about perfectly normal things. OK. Time to make sure everything's ready. Yesterday's ţuică was so good. I guess I should allow myself little things like a ţuică from time to time because man has only one lifetime. Well, after finishing here, I'll go to Mr. Sache's, and after that, I'll take the next bus. OK. It should be about time for them to pass, and if I shoot three or four, that'll be good, very good. Where are my bullets? Oh yes, here they are. Where else would I have put them? Now for the ducks—when they come, they're mine. And she, *did she really say she'd come? Why would she? What could she be looking for here? Why? Nothing all night long, or maybe she was there, she could have come to my bed and seen me sleeping in a deep trance like a zombie, and so she didn't . . . No, no, it's clear last week was a hallucination, that's all it was. But then again, on the veranda, the way she held my rifle by the barrel, oh, the hell with her, that she-devil with red hair. And in the night, the first night, she was like hot honey you wanted to be completely inside of and not know anything else. Like hot honey. Did she really say she'd come? Maybe she's here somewhere, staring at me with her green eyes. Where could she be? How strange, what is it I'm smelling? Seems like mint. How can it smell of mint here because only reeds and rushes grow here. Where can the mint be? The scent's strong as the devil! Well, on Monday, I'll tell the doctor about this problem with smells, too, and about . . . If she comes I'll know what to do with her, just let her. I'll forget about the ducks and everything else because* she, she's what I came for, *she's* the one, *oh, the hell with her and with her damned burning-hot flesh, right here, even in this place . . . Just come! Come! Did she really say she'd come? Look, oh yes, the ducks are beginning to fly by. Beginning to fly by. Here's one. OK, the rifle. Steady. Steady. Wait! There, what's in the reeds there? A fox? Oh, if it is! We won't let her get away. No, mustn't, mustn't let her get away. Let them have the ducks because I . . . What's this? A black scarf here on the cork tree? But who could have left it here? Over there, in the reeds, that red fluttering? Come on, old man, come on, after her! Let the others have the ducks. Let them. Slowly, quietly, she mustn't sense you, old man. Mustn't sense you. Easy, easy. After her! A little farther, a little farther, a little—*

"Oh, dear sir, that's how it happened," says Mr. Sache, the Village Watchman, looking down at the ground. "A great pity. But now, I'd like to heat up some more *ţuică*. It seems fitting, doesn't it?"

"Please, Uncle Sache, be so good as to warm some more," the Lawyer agrees. And while the Village Watchman trudges across the veranda in his black rubber boots, the Lawyer remembers Cristina's neutral voice on the telephone: It's up to you. It's your choice. If you have to make the trip today. You know today's the day we're supposed to go with our son to have our first conference with his teacher, to see with our own eyes how good this teacher is—anyway, what could you find out now, after more than two months, what else could you find out? Look, it's your concern. Honey, I'm coming back this evening, he'd said to her, and she, a little too formal and serious—I already told you, it's your choice. It's up to you. A feeling of discomfort came over him after he put down the receiver. And that crowd in the railway station and that uncomfortable local train. But he had to do it. Had to. Why? Not even he can fully explain it to himself. He only knows that, since a few days after he first found out, he has wanted to come here.

Mr. Sache pours the *ţuică* into the small cups and, after he drinks his own, he goes on with his story. "I whistled to the group, for us to gather, and he didn't show up. He was the only one who didn't appear. At first, I said to myself that he might have to, beg your pardon, sir, might have some human necessities, like a man. Then we counted the ducks, we had a little chat, a cigarette, and when Bald Michael arrived with his four-by-four, because he's always showing up when our work is done and giving us a short ride just to get some of the ducks, I went to see what happened. Because he hadn't come back. But to tell you the truth, not in my darkest thoughts did I imagine what I saw, Mr. Lawyer, and I'm telling you because I know you were good friends. He wasn't at the cork tree, I went looking everywhere, I shouted, Mr. Engineer, Mr. Engineer—because that's what we called him, although we knew he was a statistician, you know he told me what he was, but to me he was more like an engineer, and you have to know this because as silent and closed up inside himself as he was, I cared for him, you have to know I did.

"But nothing of him. Nothing. At the spot where he should have been, his knapsack and I don't know what else. No trace of him. Then I whistled again and the others came, too. I entered the reeds, my heart warned me of something, then I saw the tracks of his boots, and there, let's say about five feet out in the pond, there he was, so, lying face down. What are you doing, Mr. Engineer? Aren't you feeling well, my son? But he, poor man, how could he answer now? When we lifted him up from there, oh dear Mother of God, with all his chest shot away, I felt I'd pass out, although I made it through the war until the Bend of the Don, and I've seen a lot of things in my life, but I didn't know what else to do. How he could have tripped, how he could have happened to fall down with the barrel toward him, I can't tell you. He was an experienced hunter. Any child knows that you never keep the rifle, oh the hell with all of this, with the barrel toward you, never, never. Even if it has no bullet in it, you don't hold it that way. But loaded, as it was? In so many years, here in our village, there's been no accident like this one, Mr. Lawyer. Alas, then an accident happened, and happened to him. Just when he wanted to begin a new life, when he'd just begun, as men do, to have a little drink, when he'd just—such a great pity, upon my word, such a great pity. And Mr. Actor, you should have seen him, how he ripped his shirt like in those movies on TV, exactly like they do, and we bandaged the wounds with it and carried him as we could to the car of Bald Michael, who, may ravens eat his liver, kept on saying, You'll fill it up with his blood, watch it, so much blood is gushing from him. It was true, Mr. Lawyer, it was true, the blood kept on spurting all the time. But in a case like this you have to keep your mouth shut, son of a bitch this Michael was, excuse me, Mr. Lawyer, because the man was dying. Yes, the poor gentleman, he was already gone."

"But someone else, wasn't there someone else, to his right, I mean?"

"Who might it have been, dear Lord? Because his place was the farthest one, and from there on the pond began, and the swamp. There was nobody else, Mr. Lawyer. You know, those who took part in the inquiries scorned us because why didn't we let him lie there and summon them to be the first to see him. But how? Can you leave a man lying so? What if there had been some life left in him?

Should we not have carried him? Yes, of course, so we carried him, and after everything, those from the inquiry concluded *accident* because that's what it was, Mr. Lawyer, because just this long he was allotted to live in this world. But let's suppose the other side of the case, if you wish. Who could have had something against him? Look, nobody took anything from him, they found his papers, his money, everything. So what else could it have been? And with the others we would have felt something or seen something, but nobody was there, Mr. Lawyer, nobody."

"OK, Uncle Sache, I understand. It's clear to me now. Very clear. And what time did you say the bus leaves so I can catch the seven o'clock train?"

"At about half past five. But now it's a bit before five, and the bus starts from right over there, from that little bridge in front of Stan's wife's place, her name is Lena." The Watchman points out the place over the fence: a small, miserable house, a plank bridge, a bench on which a woman was sitting with her hands crossed in her lap. "She stays like that all day long. Only her daughter and her daughter-in-law do the work. Because this one, she's lost her mind, Mr. Lawyer. It's from there you have to take the bus. But you still have plenty of time."

Should he tell Mr. Sache that he'd like to see the Forest Ranger's house? Why go see it? What could he say to that man? That in fact he isn't the one he wants to see but *her,* the woman, because he must have been thinking of her and her red hair in his final hours, her green eyes that turned him, the poor Statistician, head over heels, poor man. It makes no sense. Well, is it true that it makes no sense? And if it means anything, what message does his death hold? Anyway, since he's already this far, at least he ought to see it through to the end. Because it isn't here, the end, here at Mr. Sache's, but *there* at the Ranger's, if there's to be any end. What nonsense! And yet . . .

"Is the Ranger's house far from here, Uncle Sache?"

"Here in our village nothing is far. If you want to see where he stayed overnight, my little Vasile will lead your way. Vasile! Come here and lead the gentleman to the Ranger's. Sir, you have to know that even those with the inquiry asked the Ranger if he had something to add, if your friend left a letter there or anything. But no, nothing at all. Nothing. If you want to go, please go there because you were friends."

"I'll go for ten minutes or so. Then I'll return to catch the bus. Thank you, Uncle Sache, and let's hope for the best."

"Let's hope for the best, Mr. Lawyer, because all day long we hear of the worst. Go in good health. Vasile, show the gentleman to the house."

He follows the child who is merrily running and picking up small stones from the road to throw at the geese, and he is sorry he doesn't have some chocolate with him, a piece of candy, anything sweet, to give him.

"There—" Vasile stops before a house with a porch, surrounded by a wooden fence with an open gate. Then the boy dashes away without another word, like a little wild animal.

The Lawyer's heart is tumbling and thumping in his chest. This is ludicrous, pure folly. What's the big deal? He will simply say good afternoon, explain who he is and that he wants to know if his friend said something special during the evening or in the morning before the . . . They will say no, he didn't say anything, he will thank them, excuse himself for being in a rush so as not to miss the bus, this fact is the truth, and leave. Merely to see that woman once, perhaps look into her eyes. That's all. He is about to enter the gate when a dog barks fiercely, ready to break its chain. From the house there emerges a small, solidly built man.

"Good afternoon. I was just passing by here, and I said to myself that I would, I'd like to, I might take a look here, a look around." The Lawyer feels hesitant, as if he is losing himself and getting his thoughts all tangled in his explanations.

"I know, I know. Gossip travels quickly among us. You were a friend of the gentleman, I mean the man in the accident," the Ranger says, but he gives no hint that the Lawyer should come in.

Would this man keep him there in the yard? And *she*? If she doesn't come out, if she doesn't pass by? If he cannot see her? He has to see her because *she, she's* what he came for, she's the reason, it's just for her.

"At Uncle Sache's I drank some hot *ţuică,* so if it's possible, I would like a glass of water."

"Come in," the Ranger responds, "but in my house, it's such a mess because, well, the way things are. Excuse the clutter."

The Lawyer enters, and the man pours him water from a large pitcher. While he is asking the Ranger, just for the sake of talking, what the Statistician said and if he seemed happy or sad, he looks everywhere around that room, the room of a confirmed bachelor, and tries to spy a skirt, an apron, anything, the slightest trace of a woman, but he can't find a single one. Only some unwashed dishes on the corner of a table, an open bottle of cheap local wine, a narrow bed with a striped blanket, a pair of huge black men's boots. Maybe she's in the other room, the big one—and he looks toward it. The Forest Ranger, as if he understands something from his glance, tells him, Yes, that's the room your friend stayed in, if you want to see it, you can see it. So the Lawyer stands up from the table bench where he has been sitting and enters the room following the Ranger, and in that room, a fireplace, a high bed, a small mountain of quinces on the floor, but nothing at all suggestive of the presence of a woman. The Lawyer feels a kind of pressure on his heart, a wave of bitter disappointment, a lightheadedness as if he were faint. The Ranger excuses himself for he was starting to prepare his dinner, the gentleman must forgive him if meanwhile he peels some potatoes, and they leave the room. If the gentleman wants, he can join him and share his meal, well, such as it is in the countryside, what one can get here, and he too will heat some *țuică*, and they could talk about one thing or another, and, if Mr. Lawyer would like, he could make the bed for him, the gentleman could spend the night.

"No, no," the Lawyer is quick to protest more decidedly than the occasion calls for. "No, no, I'm leaving now, on the five-thirty bus." He stands up from the bench with an unnatural haste.

"As you wish." The Ranger smiles gently. "You must know what's best for you."

"Good evening, and excuse me for all the trouble."

In fact, at this last instant, he still wants to ask him. Ask him about *her*. But how? And why? Nothing in the house betrayed a woman's touch. It had to have been a hallucination of the poor Statistician. That's what it was. At bottom what does it matter anymore? A dream. A hallucination. He steps out onto the porch, followed by the Ranger. He turns around to shake his hand. Then, over the Ranger's shoulder, through the late autumn twilight, he sees, to the left of the house and a little ways behind it, ruffled by the wind that is now rising, a field of mint.

THE GIRAFFE

HE COULDN'T FALL ASLEEP. IT WAS PAST MIDNIGHT, AND TOMORROW morning at nine would be the press conference. The symposium itself would begin the day after that. His paper was fourth on the schedule. Good, very good, Giurchescu would have said, it means they liked it, they think we've got something in our noodles, right? Giurchescu always made sure his own name came first on any paper produced by the research team, although he never lifted a finger. Doesn't everything belong to all of us? The intelligence, why should it be yours or mine or his or hers, when in reality it's ours together? In fact, however, Giurchescu wasn't what was termed a totalitarian boss. If there were four research trips abroad, one of them, the least interesting place, was allowed to go to subordinate researchers. Now it was his turn, Relu M.'s. The institute had submitted five papers to the organizers here, and they had chosen his.

When I was your age, Relu, I mean at thirty-five, I hadn't seen even a small medical spa like Olănești, and you, look, now you're going abroad for the third time, Giurchescu remarked. Take care, improve your pronunciation, bring a conservative suit with you, be sure you never look stern or gloomy, and in no case appear hunched and scowling as if over the microscope because for them, appearance counts. Politeness, casualness, self-confidence. As the song goes, *smile smile smile.* Maybe we'll succeed in landing a contract, something. And, oh yes, read slowly and with intonation.

Giurchescu felt the necessity of giving him advice—inevitably of no use—he patted him in a friendly way for two minutes as he suggested this, warned against that, encouraged him in general. Departure consisted of a lengthy and tedious ritual in which Relu M.

played along with brio and a smile on his lips. Giurchescu had said it in English: *Smile*. He kept on coaching because everything can be taught, politeness, the way to shake hands, warmth in the voice, clarity of perspective. And he, Relu M., had learned a lot since that day when, with utter amazement, he read in the institute's scientific journal, instead of his own name, "a collective led by . . ." He'd immediately dashed off to see Grecu and tell him that a mistake had slipped by, it wasn't by a collective, Giurchescu had led nothing, he couldn't understand why Grecu, in his position as editor in chief of this issue, hadn't checked it. Now, ten years later, he couldn't help grinning here in his hotel room, where the lights and the noises of this foreign city assaulted him, intensifying his uneasiness, feeding his insomnia.

For a moment he thought he'd look for the Seconal which Sanda must have put in the pocket of the suitcase. Better not. His constitution, that of a country boy who grew up never having an injection until his thirties, reacted unpleasantly to medications. Tomorrow he would feel drowsy and out of it all day, and he couldn't let that happen. Yet, despite his not sleeping, instead of being nervous because of the paper or his various meetings with the most prominent authorities in the field, Relu M. felt ravished by the same ludicrous thought, a petty episode at the seaside that inexplicably remained on the screen of memory. A little nothing, a banal scene, like dozens of others which vanished on their own because of the accumulation of new ones, new scenes as common and trivial as the ones they replaced.

To be a distance of I don't know how many miles from home, to have extremely important business to accomplish (prestigious business, Giurchescu would have reminded him), yet to be fixated like a simpleton or some kind of psychotic on a display table in an outdoor market with plastic animals heaped in disorder, a market stall under a sun that pulverized the colors, the air, the shapes, making even breathing difficult, seeming to prick the eyes until they ran with tears. Yes, the sobbing of your child, too. His words, his begging, and your own stubbornness motivated (wasn't it?) by all those books on child rearing.

If you forgot the giraffe in Bucharest, young man, it's your problem. We won't buy another. You don't need two giraffes to play with. Better a penguin, an elephant, something else. Anything else. Just not a giraffe! But yes, Michael screamed, a gilaffe! A

THE GIRAFFE

45
▾

gilaffe! I wanna gilaffe! This yellow one with bwown spots. Well, young man, we can't give in to all your silly whims. So we're not going to buy it, you repeated nervously, waiting for Sanda's approval. But she kept silent, and in her eyes you could read uninvolvement, tiredness, approval, disapproval, boredom, reproach, or, above all, nothing. Then your ridiculous speech swallowed by the incessant howls of the child, then all evening the replay of the same scene in your mind, long after the child had totally forgotten about a yellow giraffe with brown spots. Oh, what a horror! Why do they make such ugly toys? But in fact, if he had allowed him another one, well, for God's sake, wouldn't that have helped spoil him? It's not the way to educate a modern child, surrendering to all his wishes.

And Relu M., chief researcher, thought then, as he did now in the middle of the night at two A.M. in a hotel in a foreign city, about his childhood. Ah ha, how many things get solved by comparative thinking! At the age of four, he would roll a barrel hoop and run and run all day long. He had no idea that in this world there existed anything like a giraffe. And look, now he's here, and tomorrow a little flag will be placed on his desk next to a plastic placard with his name and his country's. He, who at four smeared his face with mulberries, went barefoot, and didn't have a playsuit with Donald Duck. Yes, and Giurchescu, until he was thirty-five, had never seen Olăneşti!

Really, I don't understand them, no sir, they crowded around like lunatics. Look how badly perspired I am (Sanda's father tossed on the kitchen table five rolls of toilet paper and let himself down heavily on the chair). I almost lost all my buttons. Crazy people! As if our ancestors used toilet paper. No sirree, they used corncobs. Corncobs! Or matches? No chance. They used to strike two pieces of stone together until they made sparks. And us, look at us, aping the devil's own nobility. . . .

But progress, dear Father-in-Law, what about all the progress?

Progress! he tossed back. This smog that keeps you from breathing, this plastic you have to dress in which makes you feel hot and stifled?

Yeah, comparative thinking, Relu M. thought again. It can save you or it can overwhelm you. It depends on the shrewdness with which you choose the terms of the comparison so as to make your point.

In fact, how much is a plastic giraffe? A trifle. I could afford, oh, seventy from my monthly salary. Seventy of them. From Sanda's salary as an engineer, probably seventy-five. And a child of four is a child of four.

Again and again there intruded into his mind the sound of Michael's crying, which now was superimposed on the noises of the streets. Here, people don't keep quiet even during the middle of the night. Night? What night? A little bit left. Soon it will start to turn light. . . .

From the seventh floor you could see the river. For some moments, Relu M. stared absently at the dull gray water, like a fluid boundary between reality and unreality. *Here* and *now,* two words whose meaning is never complete far from home. From the seventh floor of the hotel, the city seemed an image, a huge colored postcard he would soon toss into a drawer of his memory.

He closed the window slowly, and as he did so, the sense of embarrassment he had felt an hour before when he left the little restaurant came back with great force. He tormented himself to reconstruct the entire conversation in his mind, his feverishness and obstinacy those of a person who keeps playing back to himself the film of an unpleasant event in the hope of determining the very instant when everything slipped out of focus.

Rewind to the cool and quiet of a small restaurant with a handful of tables, very discretely illuminated, the jovial faces of the two Scandinavians, the much-too-loud tie of the Mediterranean, the Slavic melancholy in the blue eyes of the man beside him. And everyone's somewhat inaccurate French (because none among them was French) gave them a comfortable feeling of equality and a good humor, kept alive, of course, by the amber beer bubbling unhurriedly in the glasses. *Maintenant pas de problèmes professionnels. Ça va?* After the press conference (successful enough, by the way), a glass of beer was welcome.

But how had he arrived at that stupid and ridiculous story? Why did he have to tell those strangers whom he knew only through their scientific articles that he couldn't sleep the whole previous night because of the childish caprice of his own son who wanted a giraffe? *Une girafe? Oh là là* wondered the one across from him, sipping carefully from the beer's collar like white cream.

Last summer my daughter wanted a turtle. Of course I didn't buy it. We live in a small apartment that's very badly laid out, and merely the idea that such an animal could wander through my house *me faisait du mal. Comprenez-vous?* Oh no, of course not, children must not be spoiled because one never knows *comment sera-t-il demain.*

Then, broke in the other jovial man, his smile a bit chagrined, well, in fact, he had given in and bought his little girl *un petit poney, vous savez? Elle a été très malade dans son enfance* and I couldn't bear to say no, in fact my wife more than I, *vous savez, nous n'avons qu'un seul successeur.* Well, who knows what's better? But a giraffe, well, *c'est déjà autre chose.* Then Relu M. was about to try to explain to them that in fact it was about . . . but the words stuck in his throat, tickling helplessly in their borrowed, oversized clothes, paralyzed under the amused gaze of the Mediterranean fellow, crossing the resigned and melancholy blue glance of the man near him. A few moments, only a few moments were enough for him to realize the absurdity of the situation, from which he had no way out.

But if *votre petit fils* has already forgotten about the giraffe, I think in truth you have no reason to be troubled, the Scandinavian added. *Bien sur, du point de vue psychologique, c'est bien intéressant de savoir* how in the subconscious some happenings precipitate as a residue, how they grate at our nerves without any motivation. On the other hand, of course, the science of education hasn't reached the point of . . .

All the subsequent conversation passed by him, he couldn't pay attention to anything, he smiled blankly, automatically, at every sentence. *Smile smile smile.* That was all, although his sense of embarrassment had survived intact, and now in his hotel room, Relu M. stood stiffly as if he were afraid to stir up further the blood that was filling his head. Behind him, the window framed an unreal rectangle, a colored postcard that, yes, he would very soon toss into a drawer of his memory.

At nine that morning, the symposium would begin, and his paper was fourth.

He slept for a while and dreamed of a steep alley slanting upward, on which he could hardly walk, a narrow street with round cobblestones in gaudy colors and slippery as if under water. At its end he found a small store, the door to which opened slowly by itself with the barely audible tinkle of a bell. He went in as if guided by a spell. On the shelves, in perfect order, rows of plastic giraffes, hundreds of giraffes in every conceivable color. Without saying a word, the mistress of the giraffes untied the huge ribbon of a silvery box in which there was another box, and another, in which, finally, his eyes discerned the silhouette of a giraffe . . . yellow with brown spots. With unimaginable finesse, the mistress of the giraffes tied up the package again and placed it in his arms, smiling.

Then, while he was descending that narrow street, he felt the package shrink away in his arms and, with astonishment, he watched the silvery paper sides of the boxes fade one after another, falling like dry leaves. He ran faster and faster clutching in his arms the last box that soon had to melt, even this last one. He felt in his fingers the smooth back of a plastic giraffe, which gradually, on its own, became smaller and smaller. Oh, if only he could get home faster, if only this street had an end. Ten yards more, five, two, a watchman asleep in his glass and nickel cage, like a huge prehistoric insect in the frozen water of amber. A door shoved violently, and at last, the protective, secure light of a familiar space, abstracted from time, frozen, where nothing could happen anymore.

He heard just his breathing, agitated from running and over-excitement. Cupped in the palm of his hand, he held a tiny giraffe. Almost a jewel.

In the morning, Relu M. woke up content.

■ □ ■ □ ■

EVERYTHING'S OK

THIS WAS THE FOURTH TELEGRAM HE HAD RECEIVED IN THE LAST TWO years. The first was brought to him by a boy in hotel livery, on a silver tray with a white carnation beside it. The hotel's custom.

Must be from Horst, from Bern. Maybe they changed the concert date, he thought with immediate displeasure. Any modification in his schedule irritated him, and every irritation raised his blood pressure. It was only two hours before the performance, and Wagner isn't child's play.

COME HOME. MAMA ILL.

When Luigi arrived to take him to the concert hall, Luigi found him still in the armchair holding the telegram, the carnation clenched in his fist.

"*Che succede, maestro? Sta male?*"

"*No, niente, niente. Andiamo.*"

He doesn't even see the orchestra. The opening phrases have liquefied his brain. For the first time in thirty years of conducting, he hates the music. The final applause, the taxi in the rain, the airport. And in the plane, who knows why, after more than ten years, the words of that little half-crazy girl from Madrid who calculated for him the fixed stars and the ephemerides: strong life foundation, a rich psychic underground, the house of matrimony ineffectual, sensuality reinforced by a vigorous imagination, financial and emotional detachment, exceptional gift for music, powerful influence of his mother, powerful influence of his mother, powerful influence . . .

————

She was as beautiful as ever, the elegant nose, the thin lips, the royal cut of her gray-green eyes. Only very pale.

Uncle Aurel: "She had the grippe. Now she's all right. But at her age anything could have happened, even to . . . We both thought, I and your brother, that you had better come. But those good caramels from abroad, you know which ones, have you brought us some or . . ."

After the joy that overwhelmed him because he saw her alive, because he could pat her unnatural white hands deformed by rheumatism, because she too responded with tormented gestures to caress his hands in turn, he didn't care about anything else. Neither about Uncle Aurel, her younger brother, who was self-installed as head of the family after the death of her husband, nor about Victor, his own brother, the "normal" child of the family, the taciturn engineer, whom she used to love "normally"—"I could never love him as I love you, but he doesn't mind, he forgives me because you are my light and my joy and my life"—nor about Victor's two children, his nephews, sneaking more and more insistent glances at his luggage.

She caressed his hands as in his childhood, when she used to say to him, It's gone, you don't have a fever anymore, tomorrow I'll make you a rich chicken soup with tiny stars shimmering on top, and after tomorrow you can take out the new sled.

That room smelled of antiseptic alcohol now, of medicines, of old age, of the end, but he was determined to identify her scent from long ago, the best smell in the world, and look, he isn't able to, these others won't leave the two of them alone, and he'll never let himself cry in front of them because . . . "You distanced yourself from us, Gelu." And "With all these journeys of yours, you've already forgotten you still have a family here. . . . You've forgotten where you started from. We're tormented with everything here, and you, God knows, I can't at all imagine, Gelu, how an insensitive and stone-hearted man like you can make music, boy . . ."

He went on caressing her hands, weaving his fingers into her twiglike fingers, touching palms, the same way he used to do in those short moments of emotional paroxysm with the women he loved, whom he felt he possessed fully only that moment, the bitter moment when their hands joined together. That gesture, look, look where it comes from, but he didn't think about this then, not about this.

The second telegram with identical contents confused him more than the first one. Oh God, maybe this time! Maybe this time. Oh God! He told himself, It clearly must happen one day. It's part of the course of nature. He tried to encourage himself, but his words weren't enough to stop the waves of weakness which inundated him. In his hurry he forgot the score of *Walkyrie* in the Zurich airport, and on the flight he tried to picture the score, to decipher the notes in his mind, remaining immersed in it with closed eyes while waiting for the landing, but in fact it was *her* he thought about, her shrunken aged body, her gnarled hands.

When he entered the house, an indescribable bustle, a gaggle of biddies from the neighborhood fussing about, carrying pots and trays from here to there.

"He's come, Madame Iliu! The boy has come!" And then, from the kitchen door, *she,* an apron on, her hands full of dough: "Oh, Mama's Gelu." And he, stupefied, trying to understand yet powerless to understand, and, above all, no longer even capable of feeling joy.

"I didn't want them to summon you, oh your mama's dearest boy, but you know tomorrow it's Aurel's daughter's wedding, little Lia, your cousin, and, oh Mama's dear boy, your uncle Aurel said that if he doesn't write that I am sick, you aren't going to come. They want to boast about your being at the wedding because you know, you— oh, your mama's pet—you're the pride of our family, and . . . well . . . Mama's little chickie, I'm glad you've arrived. Go with your uncle, dear son, and take some money from that special account of yours, too, you know which one, and buy what's necessary from the hard-currency shop, because look at us, we're struggling to do our best, because, you know, they need a lot of things, Mama's sweet child, because only once will your cousin marry, our dear little Lia."

He let himself be dragged where they wanted, he smiled politely, he docilely answered the questions put to him by the unknown people who stared with poorly masked curiosity:

"So, are you making a lot of money, Mr. Conductor?"

"Yes."

"And do you also give some money to our country?"

"Yes, the percentage provided for by contract."

"Oh, that's good, Maestro, good. Because it's true, too true, our little country has a lot of need."

"It has."

"Good for you that you don't forget your country and your family and your poor, helpless old mother."

"Yes, yes."

After more than four years he went to the cemetery where his father lay buried. In the silence of autumn, he thought about his father, about his manner of being so alone and withdrawn, about the fact that he passed away with no noise, just the way he used to live his whole life long, about those days when, after the family gatherings, he retreated silently to a corner of the garden to smoke a cigarette and think intensely about something. About what? No, he won't ever learn because he never tried to become close to his father, to know him, to discover what was inside him. It was too late. And only here, finally, did his tears fall in quiet grief, the tears that he had to pay in debt for this journey.

As he flew back on the plane, the words of that girl came into his mind again: life foundation, powerful influence of his mother, of his mother, of . . . oh God! This sordid farce affected him so disagreeably. That he could rejoice that *she* is on her feet, that she is healthy, that *she is*!

Anyhow, something inside of him began to putrefy. To become detached. To wear away like old silk, which you can rip to shreds merely by looking at it.

The third telegram read this way:

SERIOUS FAMILY PROBLEMS. COME AT ONCE.

It was very curious that nobody said a thing to him on the telephone. And he used to call them every two weeks. They protected him, so to speak. More like, Yeah, you with your life and we with ours. Everything is the exact same way you know it to be. He couldn't find out anything, either from Uncle Aurel or from his brother Victor.

EVERYTHING'S OK

What could it be now? he asked himself, somehow already anesthetized, immune. Turned to stone? It was clear he *had to* help them, whereas they had no obligation to understand him, for the simple reason that they couldn't. "The devil alone can understand you artists!" And Uncle Aurel underscored the word *artists* with a gentle mockery, meaning, How come? Don't you have the same mother and the same father as your brother Victor? It's simply that you had all the luck, that's how come!

But did they know his genuine torments, his loneliness, masked by applause? (The women, as many as they were, could understand almost nothing, and if they wanted him, they wanted just him, not his music as well, a realization that was impossible for him to bear.) His fears, his insomnia, the ominous test results of his medical checkups, this engine in his chest which chugged along more and more arbitrarily, contrarily, exhaustedly. At least it's not the beginnings of Parkinson's. Deaf, I could continue to conduct a year, perhaps two. But not with tremors in my hands. And he watched his hands like strange wild animals, filled with autonomous life; he watched them with suspicion and worry, almost spying on them.

He'd done a lot of shopping. In order to satisfy them. At home, Uncle Aurel: "Your mother's in the hospital. She fell and they put a pin in her leg. Go see her, but don't stay long. We have some business we must attend to."

He stood at the gate of the hospital grounds about three quarters of an hour before a nurse came to let him in. He didn't ask this nurse anything. He advanced toward the hospital building, and he felt guilty. Guilty because he didn't feel himself able to tremble with worry anymore, to be frightened for her as before, because he couldn't *feel* as before, because . . . his mother is lying somewhere nearby, on a hospital bed, his old mother who . . .

"In here, Mr. Iliu."

He opened the door. In the room, only two beds. One empty, and there in the other, *she,* and beside her on a chair, the attending physician. "I kiss your hand, Mama. Good morning, Doctor, I am Gheorghe Iliu."

"So? You came at last? You let them throw me here in this hospital, like a dog, completely alone, in this room? Why did I give birth to two children and raise them and make men of them? Why? Tell me why? For them to throw me out, to put me in a hospital?"

"Don't be upset, Mr. Iliu," the doctor told him, almost whispering, leaning over him. "That's the typical reaction of old people. They feel they're being rejected. To them, the hospital is where ungrateful children abandon their parents, get rid of them. They hardly understand that certain illnesses cannot be cured at home. But they want to be at home because they want to die at home among their own. Please understand her and forgive her. Anyhow, in a week, she can be taken home. The operation went very well. Her psychological recuperation will be more difficult."

"Do you have your car with you, Gelu?"

"No, Mama. You have to stay here a while longer."

"Not even in chains. Call a taxi and, if you don't have money, *I'll* pay it. Maybe you don't have any, boy—that's why you travel all over the world, not to have any money! Call a taxi, and your mama will pay for it."

He went out dazed and humiliated, followed by the condescending smile of the young doctor.

Uncle Aurel: "What more do you want, man? She's eighty-four. She's afraid to die there. Try to understand her. What do you mean, to make yourself into a joke? Well, that's a good one! My my, how sensitive you've become, Gelu! But look, let's be practical, let's look at our real problems, in fact. Lia and her husband cannot stay with me anymore. So tomorrow you'd better go and visit some big shots and ask them about arranging for an apartment for them. And in addition, while you're there, see what can be done to speed up the official approval of your brother Victor's buying a car. Got it, Gelu? Please don't be upset, but, you know, you come so seldom, the problems keep increasing, you know, you're the sole hope for all of us, and . . ."

He stood up, lit a cigarette, and surprised himself by heading out to the garden toward that corner of his father's loneliness.

This was the fourth telegram. It had already been opened. He didn't know that the management from the hotel had sent the telegram to the clinic, and the staff from the clinic had sent it to the embassy to be translated in order to determine whether they should show it to him. Nurse Maggie, the one who brought him the music journals every day and who used to change not only his IVs but also his CDs, released his right hand, disconnected and removed the tube, and, leaving him hooked up to only the central monitor, held out the telegram for him to take in his hand and read.

"Don't worry, sir, please don't worry. It's all right. Everything's OK." She hurried to communicate this, speaking English, smiling reassuringly, adjusting his pillow. "Read it, please. Everything's OK."

APR. 25—MAMA'S 85TH BIRTHDAY.

■ □ ■ □ ■

THE EUROPEAN MECHANISM

THIS WOULDN'T HAVE HAPPENED AT ALL, NONE OF IT, IF HE HAD gone straight home that rainy November day, if he hadn't felt touched by the frail, sallow, slightly impish, footloose young man smiling sadly and leaning against the main gate waiting for some soul to attach himself to. "Come on, Mr. Pandele Sima, let's stop by the Starved Cat for a little while, have a beer, chat a bit. Maybe this rain will stop, maybe the sun will come out, there's always a better possibility, things can change."

"What could ever change, Pişti? The hell with that nonsense! You're a grown-up now. Come to your senses. It's going to go on raining."

"Pandele Sima, sir, are you trying to corrupt me by destroying my ideals? Where is that solid optimism of maturity? Well, Mr. Pandele, at least when I say that we need to lubricate the gears with some beer, I'm not suggesting anything ridiculous."

They had been sitting for a few minutes at one of the plastic tables where, from time to time, a dark, skinny waiter with the haughty expression of a minister plenipotentiary slid an order of beer without being asked (because he knew his customers), two mugs at a time of stained, heavy glass in which the liquid sloshed violently over the rim, dribbling white foam to thirsty lips that hurried to swallow it.

What might Pandele Sima be thinking of at such a moment? A vague melancholy, a kind of weak, nagging guilt that he hadn't gone straight home, a feeling that slowly made room for a similarly vague contentment that he was here, however, not who the hell knows where else, because it could be worse, couldn't it? Especially with such a rain now washing the tall plate-glass windows through which the street could be seen transformed into a river flowing in the rain, and the trees, the roofs of the buildings, which thus seemed to be sailing away.

Everything was decided that November afternoon. And although Pandele Sima, factory foreman, the new man of our socialist era, had indeed been present at all the political lessons and lectures on atheism, you still could have said that the scene floated in a medieval atmosphere, that this boy was nothing other than a strange messenger, the mysterious being ordained to bear with him the spark, there in that twilight—isn't twilight the hour of destiny?—a twilight drowned in the ancient patter of rain.

The atmosphere of the Starved Cat, the unofficial name of the category II restaurant The New Way, was fully contemporary: a miasma of cheap cigarettes and the fumes of rum, beer, and sweat. An atmosphere invaded by words flicked upward to the ceiling to drift down limp, devoid of strength, like confetti on the workers' caps, on the glorious shoulders of the first-shift assembly line, on factory foreman Pandele Sima's shoulders, and, in unconditional generosity, on the shoulders of the slender adolescent reeducated through work, the pride of the department, the only one among thirty confused youngsters reclaimed for society, rehabilitated, ren-ovated, and fully reinstalled in the ranks of the world, so to speak, through the conjoined efforts of those manifold objective factors which, as everyone can see, can and do accomplish everything.

So Pişti is the living example of what is possible, comrades, when there's understanding and good will, when the big family knows how to receive the reprobate with sympathy and dignity, and when it's made plain to him that there's nothing much worth stealing here and, moreover, it's not good to steal, anyway.

Very good. Pişti—let's be precise about this—doesn't come from some remote, poverty-stricken, socially backward village in Transylvania but from right here, a nearby village currently under-going reconstruction and urbanization—a village to which a lot of documents refer, for of course there were no controversies about the state's thoroughly planned and mandated modernization. And Pişti is undoubtedly a nickname, an invention of his. It comes from Gheorghe or from Dumitru or from Vasilica, we could look in his dossier for clarification, but would this serve any useful purpose?

"Mr. Pandele, you've got the brains to make a million. When you took only two days to solve that problem the engineer couldn't find a solution for despite trying to squeeze it out of himself for half a month, I thought, Mr. Pandele, you're a great man, it would be a pity for you not to rise above the assembly line. Now's the perfect time, I'm telling you. You've got the right stuff, the ingredients of a great man, you're twenty-four-karat, pure gold! Don't mix all day long with those mindless dolts because the danger is you'll become like them, and then you'll always be like that. Do something at the top level of your capacity, leave them with mouths agape, because you can do it, Mr. Pandele, I know you can, without any doubt."

The boy's glance flickered with a new gleam, a flame which lasted the briefest instant. Has Pandele noticed it? Did this light reach him through the curtain of smoke?

The rain has stopped completely. The tall windows now cut huge rectangles of darkness.

"Let's get going, my lad."

And that was all. By accident, Pandele Sima's hand wiped across the sticky surface of the plastic table, engraving on it a smudge, a small insignia like a snake, surely without any meaning. But at that table where he used to sit weekly, he was never seen again.

For a while Pandele didn't think about what the boy had said. Or he didn't want to think about it. He woke each morning out of sorts, went to his job, came home from his job. After about three weeks he said to himself, Enough of this, it can't go on this way anymore. Soon I'll be fifty. So far I've produced nothing worth a damn. That little devil was right. You turn stupid if you mix with the stupid. But I, if I put my mind to it, I could do something that would astonish everybody. Not mere improvements. Improvements? That's just fooling around. I'm going to create something absolutely new, something Paris itself has never seen, a mechanism that those petty engineers have never dared even dream of. I have it all in my head. That's where. I have it in my brains.

He announced at the next workers' meeting, where one had to speak about these kinds of plans, that he intended to make something of great interest to their factory, something very special, that he felt that he was capable, it would be a pity to lose his chance in life, to give up. . . . Nobody raised any objection, only it had to be described in terms of its material specifications and shouldn't cost the factory anything. In other words he could pursue this business entirely on his own but not before he completed his day's work.

His wife didn't become frightened until she saw him coming home with books. Pandele tried to explain to her that he wanted to do something extraordinary.

"You'll have the whole factory resenting you, that's the extraordinary result you'll be achieving with your damned contraption. You don't have an ounce of sense in your head if you think you'll bring them glory with your invention. One fine day, they'll kick you out, and—better know this—I'm not going to go crying at their doors. Old man, you spend money on books, good Lord, as if somebody had wrenched away your mind."

Pandele bought no other books. In fact he didn't need them. He did indeed have everything in his head.

He used to come home from the factory and lock himself in his room. "His room" in a manner of speaking, because the room belonged to his children, who now had to share one room with his wife, Vica. They were grown up, in high school, and, like any other teenagers, they were ready to accept, to believe in, and even to subscribe to anybody's craziness. Whatever others said, their father's "adventure" seemed amusing and interesting. The old man is working on an amazing thing. A contrivance, not any old kind, just of local interest. An extraordinary creation, a mechanism for all Europe!

The neighbors found out and began to get worried. What if the building should blow up? What if the machine catches on fire? The first complaint to the building committee was sent in December, a short while before the municipal stage of the contest in homage to "industriousness, inventiveness, productivity," where Pandele was obliged to present the plans for his mechanism, of course in a preliminary form which nobody could understand a great deal of. He was awarded second prize, after the trade union leader. He was content that he had the right to proceed further—to the regional stage. He understood intuitively, without comment, that he had done very well, for protocol required that the trade union leader be first with his mediocre device to make wire straight by pulling it and twisting it hot.

"We give you our fullest support and we value you to the utmost. We have the greatest expectations of you, Pandele Sima. The main thing is that you can compete at a higher level. Prepare yourself with the same degree of confidence and seriousness. We wish you health and happiness!"

After closing the executive's door, again thanking him, he came upon Iorgu Culae, from the die-making section. "Come on, Mr. Pandele, don't be dejected. These people haven't the slightest idea of what you're doing. Somewhere up above, they'll do you justice. Those higher-ups at least know how to read what you've put down on the paper. They'll recognize it, without question." Iorgu Culae was an optimist by nature.

Pandele Sima ended the winter in a state of exhaustion. His smile was subdued and his eyes had an unusual meekness.

"Just a little more. In fact, very little," he volunteered one day to his wife, who didn't dare to pass in front of his room, where, as the children bragged to their friends, the European mechanism was coming to life and where for months nobody had been allowed to enter. Sometimes Vica tried to recognize what Pandele was carrying wrapped in newspapers. What could it have been? A screw, a tube, something? But it was his business. Maybe, maybe he really did know what he was doing. Other times she couldn't help herself and pressed her ear to the door. She couldn't make sense of anything, couldn't distinguish anything. Faint noises, a rustle as of wings rubbed against one another, a kind of a sigh, a swooshing as of liquid in a pair of communicating vessels. Involuntarily, she thought of blood, who knows why, and she became frightened. She went away from the door on tiptoe, vowing that never again would she try to listen. But some days later she once more pressed her ear to the door. The same meaningless noises.

The regional stage, for reasons unknown, was postponed. It didn't matter. The contest no longer seemed to interest Pandele. His invention, that peerless contrivance, the machine that had to bring huge profits, the instrument that was to be his pride and not only his, but all owners', producers', and beneficiaries' pride, the device that would bring glory to the workers of the world, his European mechanism, was nearly finished.

"I feel there's very little left. I'll be free of it, and you'll be free, too," he told Vica one afternoon, the trace of a smile on his face. "A day, maybe two. Maybe not even that much. If not for that boy Pişti, I'd never have begun this project. He opened my eyes. To some the boy was worse than worthless, a young hooligan without the common sense he was born with, a cocky, smart-mouthed pup. But if not for that boy, ah ha, my twenty-four-karat brains would still be dry dust."

Pandele's hands, ruddy once upon a time not so long ago, sinewy and bulging with veins, now appeared scrawny, white, flaccid. He lifted them toward his wife. He touched her shoulder tenderly with a gesture that wanted to be a caress. Vica didn't know how to respond and thought it better to offer him something to eat. No, not now, he said. Later on. After.

Through the half-opened door of the bedroom the boys' voices could be heard: "The Brazilians are bound to win. They're the best."

The first day that Vica noticed her husband hadn't gone to work, she told herself, Maybe they've given him a day off because the contest was approaching.

Near evening, she called him to come eat. She had the impression that he responded with something or other, but she couldn't catch the meaning and gave up, out of fear of interrupting him just now. He had so little left.

The next day the trade union leader showed up, and, casting his eye at the door of the room where he supposed Pandele was closed in, he explained to Vica Sima that everything had a limit, the production process had nothing to do with the contest, but because of the absence of the "great inventor," none of them would be able to receive their salaries. So, for the time being, so to speak until the Nobel Prize, ha-ha, "our Edison" himself had to put in his hand and work, too, work in the factory no differently from the rest of his fellow workers.

The boss asked her to understand the situation and, pointing, get Pandele out of there, and tomorrow at six A.M. send him off to the factory.

"Did you hear, Pandele?" Vica asked the locked door after the boss's departure, slowly moving closer. Through the wood, the same indistinct noises could be heard. She knocked on the door. She rattled the handle. Nothing. A wave of fear swept over her. She flung off her apron, slipped into her shoes, and hurried out into the street.

It was warm and pleasant, a clear evening in early summer. The boys were away at their summer work program. At least they could have been home! Someone to break down that awful door. She wandered around for an hour or maybe more. She didn't feel like going back alone. She took the neighbor from the second floor with her. They entered.

"What is it, Mrs. Sima? Mr. Pandele doesn't want to come out anymore, or maybe he feels ill? Well, if you permit him to work so much! . . ."

They went closer to the door of his room. The handle turned at once. And there, in the room, they saw nobody. On the table, covered by a sheet, a kind of sack pulsed, a sort of huge stomach from which a lot of tubes and wires connected to other tubes and wires which lay on the floor, which had already invaded the bed, which had climbed up the walls.

This monster has swallowed him, the neighbor from the second floor would have liked to say, if she could have been sure that Pandele's wife could hear her or understand. But Pandele Sima's wife stood dumbfounded, pressed against the door frame, her eyes transfixed by the entrails of the machinery, mute and blind and deaf.

A week later, after the officials searched everywhere, after they came to the conclusion that the aforementioned Pandele Sima had disappeared, although without stealing any raw materials or goods from the factory where he used to work, and that he would come back when he felt like it—Yes, we'll find out what's going to happen when it happens—Vica Sima went to the factory and asked to meet with the chief of personnel.

"I'd like to speak to a boy who I know is working here in your factory. He's no more than nineteen, he's called Pişti, and he's thin, blond, and was reeducated through work."

"Pişti is a nickname, isn't it?" asked the chief of personnel. "Comes from what? From Gheorghe, or from Dumitru, or from Vasilica? Pişti and what other name?"

"I don't know," answered the woman timidly, "Pişti and nothing more. The only one who didn't leave the factory out of all those received here for reeducation."

"I don't know of any young man with this name. I don't remember any such person. And I, as you are probably well aware, I am in possession of a very complete roster of everybody. Now, concerning the purported fact that he's the only one who has remained, that's a gross error. We received thirty and of course we retain thirty to this day. People with a new dignity, reeducated by work, perfectly integrated, and, as we are accustomed to pointing out with justifiable pride, thoroughly reclaimed for society as a whole. Because, you see, although we can sometimes afford rejects in the manufacturing process, we can never afford human rejects. Anyway, about this Pişti, I have no recollection."

■ □ ■ □ ■

MR. EUGENE

WELL, TEN MILES AND WE'LL BE THERE, THE MAN SAID, TURNING THE steering wheel to make a left. I know, the woman shot back. She was dark featured and shriveled, his wife. I know, why do you think you're the only one who knows anything? I could see that mileage marker, too, and we've driven this same way for the last ten years. My memory is very good, thank you, she went on in her low voice, unexpectedly full and throaty given how petite she was, you'd better think twice if you suppose it's not. I didn't mean to imply anything of the sort, he replied, with a touch of condescension. I merely spoke out loud because I'm glad the car's running well and there's a very little ways left to the hotel. You know, these mountains are truly magnificent! I know, I can see them myself, dear. Why do you think I never see anything? I see them as clearly as you. Her reply came instantaneously. Now the man kept silent. He knew he'd better. In fact the whole trip he'd done nothing except flatter her, and instead of mollifying her, this made her more testy, but he was steeled to it, almost immune—he'd become thoroughly used to this during the past twenty-five years, no, not really twenty-five, because in the first five years things hadn't seemed the way they were now, yet how those first five years had been he himself didn't remember. It's true that of late he thought about this period many times, just to try to come up with some rationale, to explain to himself that decision of his. And then he'd arrived at the realization that the decision itself didn't belong to him, it had simply happened, a complex of circumstances in the aftermath of which he woke up one day to find himself married to this creature, with whom he'd stayed for twenty-five years, with whom he'd had one child who used to send them a Christmas card from abroad where he's been living, twenty-five years with this creature from whom he'd come to feel a sense of unbridgeable, hostile distance, although still within the bounds of civility.

He looked at her out of the corner of his eye and tried to recall her as she was *then*, there on the operating table: a girl, although she was about twenty-seven, a slender young woman both energetic and extremely principled, dedicated since the age of eighteen to her political work, otherwise a solitary bird talking in slogans and believing body and soul in what she was saying, a future brave and reliable comrade of the battlements of the new construction. A month after he operated on her, he asked her to be his wedded wife, to the amazement of everyone, because he was a handsome man, a great success with women of better social circles. He's marrying this monster to ensure his professional triumph—he accidentally over-heard the chief assistant saying—only because of this. He must think that with this woman, with her brazenness, he'll reach the top. Indeed he did reach the top, but not even now did he want to believe that the success of his medical career was due to her. Oh yes, some advantages, of course. The comfortable villa in the good residential area, his travels abroad for specialized training, maybe the positions he'd gained. But for Christ's sake, no one had performed the surgery for him! His career had been made by him, after all; it had been achieved by his own right hand, with which he himself held the scalpel. So then, why, he kept asking, why? Why had he tied himself to this woman he could never really communicate with? Not even in bed. It's true that she watched over the steady progress of his career, that she refrained from asking him when he would be home from the hospital or where he went in the afternoons. In time, he realized that he had become a precious object to her, *the* precious object she kept in her inventory, the living display which, wherever it might have been, would eventually have to come home to her. To her, the custody of this exhibit became more valuable day after day, more . . .

In the three years since she had retired for health reasons, since she had stopped working *there*—because *there*, too, changes had to be made, and none of the comrades who had shared her ideals and principled ambitions were left—she'd become irascible. She lost her former assuredness and equanimity, she telephoned him more often at the clinic, a fact that grated on him and made him beside himself, and she brought him guests, all variety of lawyers and judges, professors, connoisseurs of art. Thus in the evenings he too found himself invited as a visitor to his own house, and these people, whom he had to adopt, willingly or not, supposed that they were offering him enjoyment, lamenting all the time and asking for medical advice, grumbling about all sorts of aches and pains. And, good Lord, that amazing scene when out of the blue she rose from the table, moved near him, suddenly took his hands, and kissed them before their company, as though she were adoring a sacred relic, a most precious possession—as indeed they were to her. His hands, which held the scalpel and the surgical clamps, had for her been transfigured. He thought that his wife had gone crazy, but she resumed her place at the table with dignity and a pious, almost saintly smile. Afterward, this scene was replayed at certain intervals, always, of course, in the presence of guests, and although he felt that his head would burst, he dared not withdraw his hands. He tried nonchalantly to pass over these shameful incidents that sent the blood pounding into his head. And he understood more and more clearly that in relation to this woman, for whom he had never experienced true ardor, he had after so many years almost been forced to endure an unwonted, deeply disturbing intensity of emotion, a bitter, unsettling feeling which might be called pity mixed with disgust. The unexpected advent of this feeling became an irrevocable guarantee that he could never leave her.

In the distance he could glimpse the hotel against the clear August sky. To the left and the right—the mountains.

At the beginning, as far back as the first two years of his marriage, he had considered leaving her. But it seemed so simple a step, so natural and possible, that, well, he didn't take it. Not even when he fell in love with Mara, truly in love for the first time in his life. Not even then. He loved Mara deeply, and just because he loved her he hadn't the guts. When he told Dina about this episode, she remarked, You'll never commit yourself to a woman you love. Because of fear. You can stay only with women whom you feel as neutral about as possible. That's why your wife is ideal for you. Through a neutrality of connection. Mara would have required your soul, and you aren't prepared for such a thing, you guard against it and recoil from it. Aren't I right? He didn't answer. He wanted to answer, out of vanity, that no, she wasn't right, but he didn't have the strength to do it. When Mara told him, I'll stay with you if you marry me someday, but if not, I'm leaving with my husband, he responded, It's your business, do what you want. And she did not do what she wanted but rather what she was well-nigh obliged to. She left for America with her husband, a tedious, predictable engineer, and in fact she had no choice—because *he,* her lover, was afraid to stay with a woman he loved. After five years, when his wife, already high on the ladder, arranged for his scholarship in New York, he rediscovered Mara. Perhaps not the same one, the Mara from here, but another who seemed to carry with her the image of the Mara who used to be. He could have remained in New York. Found a medical position somewhere, at a hospital or in a private clinic. But he didn't. Because, one day, walking with Mara on the Brooklyn Bridge, he said, If I don't succeed, if I don't become the great surgeon I could have been in my own country, are you ready to jump with me from right here? Be serious, my darling, Mara answered. What crazy notions cross your mind! This was answer enough for him. And it reinforced the idea that women must play nothing more than an episodic role in his life, for pleasure—however, with no emotional or psychological expenditure. So it had been. With minor earthquakes, small disruptions, more or less harmless, at an inconsequential level, far in the background. Now it was a little harder for him. Now when this girl Dina was his right hand and his confidante for her two-year residency. This girl whom he cared about with mixed feelings: a sort of paternal care, an excruciating tenderness, an undeniable recognition of complete psychological and physical compatibility. Because Dina, something so rare for her generation, was eager to learn. From the first operations he sensed it—with a touch of exaltation and psychic instability in his realization. A perfect partner—truly the one person to whom he could speak freely, unreservedly, about anything.

A mere hundred yards or so from the hotel, he can't help thinking of Dina, as always with a sort of agonized joy, an unplumbed inner desolation. Dina, who gave up everything for him and moved into a one-room apartment in the remote White Pond district near the edge of Bucharest. And he, who, as he had been doing for years, went out of town with his legal wife, this strange creature, just to fulfill the duty of their annual ten-day vacation at the same hotel, where he has to sleep with her in the same bed, to feel her breath, that promiscuous heat which humiliates him and embarrasses him almost beyond endurance. He knows he'll never have the strength to . . . He knows everything will go on as usual. Above all, he knows that Dina will be accepting because nothing humiliates her or demeans her. If only he could make a break, start over again. . . . But what for? It's already getting late. Too late. Perhaps it's better this way. For sure, for sure, it must be better this way. This was meant to be. But maybe still, despite all of this, if he had the guts, if . . . No, it's not about that, it's about time. And he, he has no more time. It's better this way, far better. Because it's very late.

It was already midday when they arrived. The hotel, the same for all the years they'd been coming here, despite a couple of petty and useless improvements: some umbrellas over the tables on the terrace on the right side, a huge billboard on which were listed, absurdly, what it called "advantages of the mountains." They parked the car, took out the luggage. Near where they were entering, an elderly gentleman, maybe seventy-five, sitting in hiking shorts on a folding camp stool, raised his eyes from the huge pack in front of him, into which he was stuffing the various objects that lay in disorder on the steps, and informed them with unexpected gravity, Tomorrow I'll be ready, tomorrow I'll climb the mountain. The doctor felt obliged to smile approvingly, but she, after passing the old man and entering the poorly lit lobby, observed in a loud voice, A lot of madmen in this world, too many. Why do you say this, my dear? he asked. Why? Didn't you look at him? What mountain? That man, could he climb a mountain? And his expression! I know madmen from their expression.

The room where they had to stay ten compulsory days, time for her to rest from the hubbub of Bucharest and for him to protect his golden hands, was clean and nice and smelled of fir. From the balcony of their room, the nearest mountain seemed so terribly close.

They went on small excursions every day. In a youthful spirit she picked alpine flowers, which she forgot in the dining room. They spoke very, very little to each other. In fact, they had come to rest, hadn't they? Especially in the evening, the bluish fog, the serenity, the quiet, the vista of the mountains troubled him, and he felt a knot in his throat. He would sit by himself on the balcony looking for hours at the mountain and thinking of that girl, which he couldn't do in his wife's presence, and he promised himself, OK, this has gone on long enough, it's over. When he returned to Bucharest, he would try, try to—"Come inside, Victor, your hands will freeze. Come on, tomorrow is another day." In the morning, after tea with bread, butter, and marmalade, they went out for some fresh air. Near the entrance, on the steps, waiting for them and the few other guests, the old gentleman with his obsessed eyes, his sudden gestures, and the unvarying sentence that took the place of good morning and good evening and everything else, Tomorrow I'll climb the mountain.

At their departure, Ilie Cristescu, the manager, escorted them to their car, as he had every year. After they passed by the old gentleman, the manager felt himself obliged, for no particular reason, to confide in them: That's Mr. Eugene. He's been coming here for fifteen years, usually in September. This is the first time he's come in August. For fifteen years—fully prepared, everything he needs. You won't believe me, dear madam, he has the ropes, the harness, the carabiners, pitons, and piolets, boots with crampons, everything. He takes them out of his pack, cleans them daily; he polishes them, puts them back. Yes, yes, said Mr. Cristescu, looking back at the old man while they were fitting their luggage into their car, have a nice trip. I look forward to seeing you once again next year. I'll stay right here with Mr. Eugene and these mountains. Don't concern yourselves about him in the least, that at his age he would dare to . . . good God, no. About that you can rest assured. Mr. Eugene has been saying the same thing every day for more than fifteen years when he comes here. Tomorrow? No, he'll never do it.

■ □ ■ □ ■

THE GRAND PRIZE

HE DIDN'T RECOGNIZE BEETLE AT FIRST. AND HOW COULD HE HAVE recognized him, so very plump, with his mustache flowing downward over the corners of his mouth, with his Buffalo plaid jacket ready to split at the seams, with the beginnings of baldness unsuccessfully hidden by the hair combed upward from the sides of his head? Who would have said twenty years ago at the graduation banquet at the university that the tall, slender, handsome boy, whom half of the girls in philology were chasing after, would someday resemble this pudgy, double-chinned, already half-bald individual? And that he would not just resemble this person but would *be* him. These things happen after twenty years. Some turn fat, others get lean and hollow cheeked, still others die. Whoever decides to come to a reunion must be prepared for everything. And concerning the girls, better not say anything. About them there was a real sadness, not to mention a tragedy.

All of them were kissing one another in a natural effusiveness (some of them hadn't seen each other since then, when they were assigned their jobs upon graduation), without fully knowing who was kissing whom.

"Hey, I'm Doina, man. Don't you recognize me? I can't believe it! Give me a compliment, tell me I haven't changed a bit, so I can slap your face like I used to slap you in the second year of comparative grammar when I failed the midyear exam because of you. It's me, Doina, man, and she's Luci. My dear, don't tell me you didn't recognize her from the first look, because I'm already losing my confidence in men."

Yes, she was Luci indeed, the skinny girl (girl?) with thick, convex lenses over her eyes and blue shadow on her eyelids (oh, her eyes, yes, of course, there's no way Cristian could have forgotten those eyes which made him lovesick for an entire summer during practice teaching in Cobadin).

"As if, dear," Doina went on, "you think you look the same? And don't stare at us all befuddled because you'll give us complexes, and if we kiss each other, peck peck, in a friendly way, let's first of all know who we are. So come here, mister, I can introduce everybody because I have a particularly sharp memory. If you want, I can tell you by heart the first three lectures in Old Slavonic, and in dialectology, and in whatever other courses you didn't used to take notes in because you borrowed mine, already written by this little hand which, look at it, how it's swelled up these days from washing diapers and men's underwear and all sorts of other not particularly philological or aesthetic matters which over the span of twenty years must be untangled by an intellectual woman with her pretty little hands, yes sir. Because, Mr. Editor in Chief, sir—that's the way they must address you when they come to you with their play scripts for you to tell them yes or no, and what about this problem with the positive characters and the not very positive, and with the plot, the conflict which must be but, at the same time, must not be . . . and with . . . well, let's drop it, the problems with the dramaturgy in general—because I myself read your articles in the Romanian press, I don't have access to any other. So. That's how it is in a small provincial town. Well, do they know, those who come to you, do they know what a slacker you were at the university, what a bramble thicket you had inside your curly little head, you couldn't distinguish this from that, and that from anything else? Do they know what a scared conformist, what a sweet little mouse Mr. Editor used to be, who today has such courageous literary opinions, and not only literary? Because, well, as you see, some of us still keep on reading, what else can we do? We still keep on reading, I mean we who are swallowed up alive by the provinces."

Yes, that was surely Doina. Bracing. The same as twenty years ago. Sarcastic, feisty, sincere, always helpful. Funny, too, and conscientious. And what more? Oh yes, one hell of a sweet girl.

When they came upon Beetle, Doina stopped for a moment, pursed her lips, narrowed her eyes (exactly the way when, at the university, she was ready to make a crucial point but first she studied you for a few seconds to judge how to be more effective). "Cristian, I think you recognize your good friend Andreescu, called the Director, called Beetle. It would be more than likely you recognize him though disguised in this fashion by his mustache and his pleasing hint of baldness. Because surely he recognizes you. What do you say?"

Beetle at once embraced Cristian in his arms, kissed him with a smacking sound on both cheeks (Beetle smelled of pipe tobacco and Chess aftershave), stepped back to take a better look at him from top to bottom, circled him, and again stood in front of him with his feet apart and hands behind his back like Napoleon.

"Bravo, old man," Beetle exploded at last, "you've accomplished all that you've accomplished, but you didn't get older, not even a second. That's some achievement. Look at us (excluding the girls, of course, because it's very normal that they must never get older) and then look at you. No belly, no baldness."

"Ah yes, but his importance has grown," Doina (who else?) interrupted. "I think you realize, dear Beetle, that this distinguished gentleman, our dear colleague, is a sort of a big shot. It would have been a great pity for him not to have made it after he worked so hard at becoming one of the bosses. Why shouldn't we have someone to be proud of? From the common and amorphous mass of professors and librarians and pedagogues whom we have turned into, there has emerged our strongest shoot, our representative, the first of our class, the distinguished Cristian Grecu, who today grants us the honor of appearing amongst us in blue jeans and without a tie, free, casual, cool, not like you in dark suits and white shirts, you provincial people, awkward and emotive. Can you, Beetle—tell me—can you detect a crumb of sentiment in this honorable man? No, you don't see a hint of one. You don't, because he has none. Our distinguished editor is trained like a cosmonaut. And not merely since yesterday or the day before."

Doina rattled on with huge enjoyment. Her words had a kind of wistful aggressiveness, which she probably wasn't quite aware of—because what reason could she have now, here in a restaurant (category deluxe), rented for the evening, for this sort of comic-ironic assault with no effect other than the eventual discomfort and embarrassment of everyone?

"Hey, come on, it's not really that way," Beetle said to repair the atmosphere, as if he would reply, Doina, don't you see that he's a human being himself? I mean, he seems to be one of us. After all, he came here. "How could he not have feelings? All men do after twenty years, in such a situation as this."

"Of course he does, too," added Doina. "It's just that he's afraid to be asked for something because, you know, this is a big problem for bigwigs. Their most unpleasant relationship is with their former colleagues and old friends (in the event that in their youth they could have been imprudent enough to make friends deficient in future importance). They're worried that these former friends will appeal to them for one thing or another. Didn't you see it on TV? There were some comic skits on this theme."

Doina burst out laughing. She had a contagious laugh like a waterfall, the tonic laughter of a healthy and self-confident person.

"I hope you didn't lose your sense of humor forever, sir. That would be truly tragic, let me tell you, tragic for you, too, to be like the majority of those people who, upon being 'anointed,' find themselves in the same instant deprived of their humor and their normal reactions. As if humor and normal reactions would be nonconformist, detrimental to standard development. But in relation to me, dear Cristi, don't be concerned. For, insofar as my turning, on the spot, irresistible again and forever ingratiating, I must inform you that I don't have the least intention of ever asking you for anything. Because I don't need anything. I have two children, I have a house, I have a bank loan, I have an advertised, modern Alba Lux 2 washing machine, I have an asphalt road, running water, electricity, if I want to go to Iaşi I have an express train to the city once a day, I have a youth group, I even have some responsibilities because I'm group leader for the Young Pioneers and I'm in charge of the Party bulletin board at work, I have plastic curtains with red poppies in that classroom where I'm the grade principal, every summer I get to go for free to the Navodari campground on the Black Sea, I have a freezer—do you have one? you see, you don't?—I have such nice prospects: I'll spend the New Year's holiday in Bulgaria, I'll earn an honorable mention with the Young Pioneers brigade at the Festival in Praise of Romania, I'll buy a fine rabbit-fur jacket and new-fangled door chimes that *bing-bang-bong-bing,* I'll have a winning ticket in the state lottery. What more?! I'm a contented individual, and I don't need anything more because, if we add the least thing to this immense, vast happiness. . . . So you see, my sweet Mr. Editor, you can rely on me. I'm the most comfortable friend in the world, the ideal friend, the one who never asks for anything. And now, are you hungry? Let's go eat. Because I feel that my energy is flagging, and if I lose my energy, I'll lose my charm, and without my charm . . ."

The table was arranged in the shape of a U, as for weddings and all festivities of the kind. Along the table's short (and official) middle leg the professors were seated, those who were still alive, those who had resisted the flu, official restructurings, senate meetings, earthquakes, arteriosclerosis, heart attacks, changes of temperature and pressure, the winter wind from the steppes, the spring thaws. Twenty years during which the wind blew however it would blow, sometimes from there, sometimes from other places, said Cristian Grecu to himself. Twenty years while some of them got older like the assistants, some others—oh ho!—became lecturers and professors, and others went further, some of them very high up, everyone with his or her own particular destiny.

Who could guess that this shriveled little man, with parchment-like skin and red, congested eyelids, all the time beaming with equal warmth at his former students (whom, it must be said, he couldn't distinguish from other former students), at the waiters, at the tablecloth, at the festive fir tree branches, is the very initiator and tireless leader of the celebrated campaign against "good morning," the same personage who more than twenty years ago filled all the Romanian newspapers with his argument against this most banal greeting. The phrase "good morning"? It implies mysticism because wishing someone a good morning, on the one hand, means you admit that a supernatural force makes a morning good, and on the other hand it means you have doubts about that truth according to which our days cannot be otherwise than serene, happy, and full of promise. And therewith, dozens of articles from which other archaisms didn't escape either, "good luck" or "here's to your health" and similar formulas with roots in that obscurantist past with which our people had to make a break forever in order to be able to advance freely in the direction necessary for progress. And Comrade Professor suggested the replacement of "good morning" with other more vigorous and forward-looking formulas, more revolutionary, clearer, which after so many years he himself has thoroughly forgotten and hopes that everyone else has forgotten as well. Because people have become used to forgetting stupidities easily. At first they wonder, then they resign themselves to things, then they forget under the pressure of some newer and bigger stupidity, in a perfect dialectical progression. Now R.H., beaming, sits benignly at the head of the table among those in the position of honor.

Beside him looms the deputy dean's portly wife, with her round face screwed up in an imposing triple chin like an Elizabethan collar, her countenance a smooth wax mask interrupted by the firm, thin line of her mouth—a straight line like in children's drawings. For her sake a young engineer had thrown himself from the second floor! For her!? (Let men likewise commit suicide out of love, Doina had remarked then, when all the university had roared. It's very good for them to become so sensitive, for them to cut their veins, take poison, throw themselves onto the train tracks. Long live Werther's nephews!) The engineer hadn't died. He fell down—I don't know how—on something and then rolled onto something else, so he was left with a metal rod in one leg, definitively cured of the passion in his heart.

And Mr. Deputy Dean, what was he doing during that period? Indeed, what he did was to confront head-on the class character of language, that is to say, the incontrovertible fact that the language of the people was one thing but the language of the oppressors wholly another. And taking into consideration the truth that the exploiting classes lack character, one can say that their language likewise is of a piece with them and their well-established deficiencies. Is this clear? Of course it was clear. Convincing, too. It had to be.

Less clear seemed to be the problem concerning great writers' language because, unfortunately, not all of them came from the lower class, some among them derived from the landowners, princes, bishops, and the like. About this issue the various factors seemed to be more muddled and contradictory. Ah, only *seemed* to be, because Comrade Deputy Dean never let himself be intimidated by recalcitrant reality, and in the end he always succeeded in fitting actuality into the organized and systematic framework of that theory which allows no deviation. A short time afterward, the great specialty of the deputy dean developed into the ferreting out, the identification (a result of that action Doina termed a "dark quest by candlelight") of no fewer than three impoverished relatives in the family of every great writer, from whom he extracted "the good sap of the true language" because it's impossible, isn't it, not to discover even for an aristocrat like the nineteenth-century playwright Alecsandri, somewhere on his huge genealogical tree, at least one stunted branch, a "downtrodden, oppressed, but healthy element," as Comrade Deputy Dean was fond of proclaiming, to establish as its necessary heritage "the true and vital language of the masses."

All this blossomed again for him in Cristian Grecu's smile, oh yes, he had memories, too, not only Doina Stăncescu (by the way, what was her married name?). These, and others from the same period, the "obsessive" decade, some were calling it now—what a joke! Why was this period any more obsessive than any other, than the whole century, the whole millennium? Cristian Grecu asked himself, absently chewing meatballs and sausages. Each age with its unique obsessions, or rather with its fun, if you know how to break from the past with a grin, and this, the best solution—for preserving your nerves— didn't originate with him. But he'd adopted it rapidly and most use-fully ever since he stopped being a student. . . .

Should auld acquaintance be forgot
And never brought to min'? . . .
We'll tak a cup o' kindness yet,
For auld lang syne.

Everyone stood up, he stood, too, his vodka in his hand, clinked glasses with the blond beside him, Simu's wife, and with Simu, and with the engineer on his right (it seemed he'd said he was an engineer), Luci's husband, and with Tomescu, and with Picu:

And let's live it up, my dear, let's see each other more often, why not in five years, why wait to wear out completely? . . . Are they your children, Luci? So big? Enjoy them. But you must see mine. No, I have no photos with me. I left in a hurry, directly from the auto mechanic's service, because on Thursday someone hit my car. Yes, a lot of money. They still get away with it, no restraints, they went so far as to help themselves to the jack from my trunk. Oh, hell, it's small! For what? Damn baksheesh! Is someone to pay me more than my salary? No, no, I'm not going to agree with you about this despicable Balkanic habit. You can't even buy a book without tipping. . . . I have a cousin who works there. Since they began making freezers, he hasn't answered my calls. . . . Principles? What kind of principles, man? . . . First you could hear a noise, then it made a loud clunk, then it didn't go at all. . . . Thirty-two hundred lei, a fortune. . . . Despite their three, they're good for nothing because you have to go from one to another, they won't help, and my mother-in-law lives there, too, so you can imagine . . . The supervisor said it's unacceptable for four of them to have to take a repeat examination in Romanian because this is our common maternal language and it's impossible that it not be known to every Romanian by heart, and he punished *me*, he yelled at me, only in the worst grammar, and in the end he said that he would forgive me "for the momentary," but this was never to be repeated, never, and all I could do was go home crying and . . . Well, that's the way it is with the people, so let's march in the parade alongside them. . . . Beer makes me feel sick. Vodka. That's the stuff. . . . Impossible, man, you can't be knowledgeable about everything, not even during the Renaissance, not even Leonardo da Vinci, who . . . And he, no, no, no, and no again, until I got ticked off and I said, hey you, you're so clever, you'd better realize that rock 'n' roll wasn't invented by you. We, we're the Beatles generation, we who're now in our forties.

A moment of thrilling silence settled over them. Who was it who spoke about the Beatles? Picu? Tomescu? Beetle? It doesn't matter since everyone there feels a kind of weariness, something like a wave coursing through the neck and curling there in a painful knot. Let's cure it with vodka, let's cure it with beer, let's cure it with something. It can still be cured. It'll go away . . . "Yesterday."

"Adrian didn't come. Does anyone know anything about Adrian Lascu?" Luci's voice was small, tremulous, hesitant, as always. "None of you used to dance like him. Do you remember? He was extraordinary!"

"We were colleagues at the institute for about three years," said Picu. "Then he left for a year abroad for advanced study. It's a long story about Adrian. I saw him a month ago. I visited him at the hospital."

"The hospital? What's up with him?" Tomescu asked.

"That's the point, because it's nothing definite they can put their finger on," Picu went on. "I spoke with him for nearly an hour. He was absolutely coherent, but his wife indicated that the doctors want to keep him there for at least a month. He has good moments and moments of depression. I was lucky. I caught him in a good phase. He was calm and somehow detached from the story which explained his stay in the hospital. For you to understand at least some of this, it would be necessary for me to tell you about the atmosphere in our research institute, but I don't have the energy for such a long story."

"Oh, come on, man, what in fact happened?" Tomescu asked again. "What have you done to him?"

"That's the whole point, nobody did anything to him or, to be more accurate, nothing I could discern at all. Anyhow, nothing concrete. Do you understand? I mean he wasn't kicked out, nobody took credit for his articles and signed them instead of him, nobody put roadblocks in his way when he needed to go abroad, there was nothing at all. All was going well. Very well. Too well, maybe, those in his department used to say. He married a graphic artist, a talented and gorgeous woman whose father used to keep bees, they had a nice child, they bought a car and then a house, he won a scholarship for one year in England, and after he returned home, he was made a principal researcher; by the time he was thirty-five, he already had two published books and was awarded the academy prize. Then a rumor started to circulate throughout the institute that Adrian had somebody backing him, because otherwise it's impossible, everyone knows, to rise so fast. I heard these whispers myself, but most of the time they kept things like this away from me because they knew we used to be students together at the university. It's impossible, you know, that he doesn't have someone 'sponsoring' him, said Mrs. P.M. (the one who has the weekly TV talk show). There are other very capable researchers, others who work hard, and others, too, who are correct, congenial, good-looking, yet they haven't made it as far as this Adrian Lascu. His wife doesn't cheat on him, his child is winning honors in school, he's healthy, he has no professional disappointments, he never complains about money—something's not right here, she said. But she wasn't the only one who said so.

"After a while, and this was to be anticipated, the rumor reached Adrian's ear. At first, he had no reaction (he told me this himself at the hospital when he tried to explain to me what happened and how). Some time later, he began to feel obsessed by the whole business, and next he questioned himself: *Do* I have someone supporting me behind my back? Suddenly it occurred to him that everything in his life was going exceptionally well, when he thought in fact that his life was just going normally. X was in court with his former wife to divide their possessions. Y couldn't succeed in writing a minimally acceptable doctoral thesis. Z's boy gave up the university for a ballerina who convinced him to become an auto mechanic. Well, everybody around him in fact had troubles, temporary and commonplace human worries in the end, not tragedies, but, anyhow, enough to make them apprehensive, to make them bitter, to give them complexes. During this time he, Adrian, came to feel (he confessed this to me at the hospital) like an unreal character kept in an aseptic vessel by a novelist who wanted on purpose to introduce into a normal story, full of living and plausible characters, a hoax, a puppet, a false type, a positive hero from *a* to *z* with no defeats, no failures, no shadows or nuances, the symbol of a thesis about happiness in vitro.

"Everything in fact derived from this question he became obsessed with because, you all know Adrian very well, he wasn't content only to note his doubts. He undertook, you won't believe this, his own 'investigations'—this is the exact word, and it's his. Not immediately. For a while he didn't do anything particular. He still had intervals, he said, when he told himself that if there really was someone backing him, it's this someone's business as long as he himself feels all right and no one asks for anything in return from him. But if one day it turns out that he's going to be asked for anything, if one day a deadline passes and someone informs him, That's it, little boy, it's your turn now, if he weren't ever going to be able to pay (or wouldn't want to) because who knows in what kind of 'money' he'd be asked to pay. . . . Anyhow, Adrian said there in his hospital room (where we were talking all the time, the nurse never once stepped out), a perfect, A-plus life, without family conflicts, without professional failures, without missteps and misfortunes, I don't think that could have been paid for (if it came to anything like a bill) with merely a smile and a sincere thank-you from the bottom of my heart. Who knows what kind of smell, taste, and color that wad of bills would have that I could be asked to pay with?

"You have to realize that I didn't interrupt him and that I didn't try to tell him *then* that he needed a period of R and R, a vacation somewhere in the mountains, or that he should have talked to someone, a friend who might have comforted him or might have told him, in practical terms, Look here, Adrian, if your life's an A plus, it's because you're a top-grade A-plus man, because you're gifted and serious, and because it happened to be you who had this luck, oh yes, this opportunity and nothing more, this chance for everything to be all right for the time being. Don't drive nails into your own coffin, you've no reason to. I said nothing like this because, anyhow, it was too late, nothing would have mattered. And he went on telling his tale in such a fever, he was so 'absorbed' in it that any interruption of mine, even of approval, might have upset him, and that nurse, glued to her chair in the corner of the room, seemed to be waiting for such a thing to throw me out."

"Well, what did Adrian do? Did he immediately get put in the hospital? His nerves went bad, all of a sudden, because of a fanciful supposition?"

"Oh no. In fact this isn't half the story. Because, as I already said, he didn't stop at this point, I mean noting all this and tormenting himself. He undertook his 'investigations.' I couldn't understand exactly what he meant by 'investigations' or what he actually did, but it's for certain that after some months of research with no result, I mean without coming any nearer to identifying 'the man in the shadows,' the secret someone who arranged for his success—and I think you realize what kind of expense of psychic energy such a quixotic undertaking implies—Adrian realized that his man purely and simply didn't exist. Well, a normal assumption, we ourselves would say now, in our tranquility and with clear minds. And still more normal it would have been, after such a determination, for him to calm down and mind his own business like before, since backing Adrian Lascu, was, it turned out, nobody other than Adrian

Lascu. As for myself, such a conclusion would have strengthened me. But Adrian, instead, was crushed, destroyed. Thus his fears kicked in, his hesitation, his downfall. Nothing worthwhile came from him anymore, he couldn't concentrate, he became irascible and unfocused. His colleagues from his department said, 'What's with this Lascu fellow? Has he fallen in love? He doesn't know what world he's in any longer. He didn't finish his research paper by the deadline, for the first time in twenty years. He's also lost files which can't be replaced'—well, lots of things like these, a whole chain of them. Then I stopped working there, so for a long period of time, I wasn't up-to-date. I heard about much of this in random details from a mutual friend, the same one who by chance later let me know that Adrian was in the hospital. This is the way it was with Adrian Lascu. He was always a little bit, how can I say it—'strange.' Do you remember that time when we were in our third year at the university, the story of the vote, with—" And Picu broke off suddenly at the very moment that he realized that Cristian Grecu was right in front of him—oops! he was about to commit a bad faux pas, if he hadn't already—so he finished all in a rush, "Well, he'll get better and then we'll have a big bash to celebrate, but before then, let's hoist a glass to his health and rattle our old bones a little. What about it, Luci, shall we dance? Baby, let's shake it. I don't dance like Adrian (I couldn't do that twenty years ago, either), but if we give it a try and press ourselves together a little bit . . . I hope your husband won't get the wrong idea, it's Mr. Engineer, isn't it?"

"Go ahead, take her, man, take her, I let you have her openheartedly," the engineer said, laughing, "because, as for myself, I've never danced in all my life, and this is only one of five hundred weak points of mine that my wife already knows by heart. I'm the man with the production, with the plans, with the engines. Dance as long as you wish, and as for me, if I have a small glass in front of me, I feel all right, even here. Here someone like me can talk with people in the best circles, I'm getting more cultivated myself, because we engineers don't have much time to read—not like you, who went to a college for reading novels—a pleasure, sir, to read novels and poems, and to get a university diploma for this, and to see your name in the papers. Right, Mr. Grecu? Excuse my question—you know, I've never been in contact much with people like you—do you also get paid some money for what you write in the newspaper, I mean beside your salary? Because you know, we work in the factory until our eyes pop out of our heads. . . . Well, you know, since you're a former colleague of Luci, I can permit myself to ask you is it true that writers are rolling in money? Or is this a mistaken opinion?"

"Wrong, mister, wrong." Cristian Grecu cut him short—the engineer had already begun to irritate him. How lucky that Luci wasn't there because otherwise she would have felt mortified.

"And unless it shouldn't be this way, the way I've already told you I've heard about," the engineer persisted, "you know, I'd like to start to write myself. I bet I could do well, by God, because our Romanian language couldn't be more complicated than mathematics! 'Cause this Romanian language, as it's said, we all know it, all of us— and in this respect I myself agree with that supervisor someone here was talking about previously. But I didn't want to enter the discussion because it's not nice at a festivity like this one to contradict someone, it seems to me, so that's why I kept silent. What do you say?"

Cristian Grecu said nothing. He raised his glass of wine (Great Hill label, pretty good!) and drank it slowly in small sips. He was on the verge of anger (not only because of the engineer), and he didn't at all want his ulcer to start bothering him again. That ulcer he could date to that senate meeting when he and Doina and Adrian *had to* vote, that meeting Picu has never forgotten, nor Doina, nor, probably, any of them.

"And let me tell you that I have good subjects for a novel," the engineer droned on. "Yes. A lot of them. From the maintenance department to the chief mechanic. I could even write a play. I haven't tried so far, but if I practice it a little . . . because, as you know, I have no training in writing with letters, ha-ha, because we, you know, we're much better with figures. That's the profession. But if you say so, that you don't make a lot, hmm," the engineer continued, look- ing at him in disbelief, and his eyes seemed to say, Don't try to trick me, I heard what I heard and there's no use telling me no if it's yes because I don't intend to run off with your share, after all we're both human beings. "Take, for example, yes, here's one, there's a guy, a Mr. Plum, the chief of the team. This man is a hell of a character! This guy always says that everything he does is perfect, and you can protest as loudly as you want that he fucked up because he, no, no, no, and this particular guy has, man, astonishing explanations that will stupefy anybody. All the rest are afraid when they deal with him. But it's not enough for him to know that the others are afraid, no, he wants them to love him, believe it or not. And he tortures them as if they were horse thieves. And they caught on to this weakness of his, and they keep on saying, Mr. Plum, there's no one in the whole factory braver and more efficient than you, God himself chose you specially because if we were by chance on Mr. Săndulescu's team or Mr. Tică's team, we'd be nothing, like dust. And this Plum, what do you think he does then? He strikes his own people from the list of bonuses. And then this Plum, he comes to me satisfied, and I ask him, Why, Mr. Plum, why? They're your own men. Let them be, he says, so they'll know fear of me, let them know that here, *I* am their father, because if you don't keep a tight rein, they'll think they've been let loose in the field and won't work at all, and then the hell with the plan and bonuses. Let them be afraid of me and thank me from early morning to bedtime because Plum's the one, I'm making real men out of them, and I know they love me, much more than any bonus, they love me because I'm the way I am, I'm their father, the one and only Plum. And I, I make the mistake of telling him it's actually the opposite. Mr. Plum, these men go around all day long cursing you behind your back because if you cut someone's money, that someone will never forget you their whole life. And Plum turned red with fury—because it's impossible for anyone not to love him, and he'll show them, screw these villains' mothers! And from then on, he treated me no differently from them, and during the next Party meeting he said that I was at the most rudimentary level of political education, and moreover I'd been married twice, and this and that in addition—what can I say, he painted me so prettily that, when the conclusions came to be summarized and it was my turn to speak, I couldn't say anything except to tell them, all this is enough, comrades, as for me, I myself agree with everything, we're in total unanimity.

"Oh, and others, too, especially good for a novel because this Plum, he's really something, a real piece of work. You know, no more than one month ago, the leader of the Union of Young Communists came to me, his pale face like fresh whitewash, and told me, almost speechless in amazement, Comrade Plum has fallen ill. He has swollen glands. That's to say, dear sir, what an infamy, ill-ness doesn't have a solid criterion upon which to dare touch our Comrade Plum in the slightest. That's it, sir, why should we add anything else? They love him, they love him boundlessly."

Cristian Grecu felt he was suffocating. He had to find some pre-text, any excuse, to flee from the vicinity of this future novelist or playwright or whatever he wanted to be, to dance with a girl, to go to the toilet, to escape anywhere else. He stood up firmly, cast his eyes all about the room, as if searching for someone, and then said politely, "I have to exchange some words with a former colleague who couldn't arrive earlier because he lives in the far north, near Sighet. I'll come back and we can go on with our discussion."

"But do you think that this Plum would be good for a character? If not, I have others, many more, who . . ."

"No, I'm sorry, I don't believe he'd be very good." And he let issue forth that saving sentence heard at the last editorial meeting: "He's a peripheral character. In fact, without doubt, he's in no way typical of our society. He's an isolated case. Anyhow, any story that could have at its center such a, let's say, a caricature would have no mes-sage. And without a message . . ."

"Message? What kind of message should there be, man? What message?" the engineer repeated, with a totally confused face.

"Well, that's the very problem, that's it!" Cristian Grecu threw back to him enigmatically, going courageously to the men's room.

It was already nearly eleven. By one o'clock this tale will have to come to its conclusion, Cristian Grecu said to himself, searching with his eyes for a place to sit a few minutes, anywhere other than next to the engineer—to breathe awhile, to let the engineer calm down. He felt caught by his arm. He turned his head. It was Beetle.

"Could we talk together quietly for two minutes?" Beetle asked, smiling somehow embarrassedly, as if he feared a denial or a delay.

They passed through the pairs of dancers and went out to the ter-race. It was a clear June night, with an occasional breath of wind. Cristian Grecu tripped over an upside-down chair, and the violent pain in his knee added to his bad humor; whatever one might say, he didn't feel at ease.

"Damn it! They don't have any light here. You can crack your head open."

"As long as we have stars, and look how big they are, it's the best time to economize on electricity," Beetle laughed.

They sat down in the right corner of the terrace, as far as they could from the racket inside. They sat in silence. Grecu felt his heart constricted, he was overcome by a vague feeling of discomfiture. He waited for Beetle to begin. But Beetle said nothing. He methodically filled his pipe, staring hard to see it under the feeble natural light of the stars—a few of them big stars, like in the scenery of an operetta. Unreal. False.

"I'm going to get two glasses, so we won't sit here dry. I'll be back in a moment."

Beetle stood up and Grecu gazed after him as he went away, with a sense of release (yes, release—any delay is a release in such situations), until he watched him push aside the velvet curtain that hid the door to the terrace and he registered, for a moment, the wriggling of the people inside, his fellow students from twenty years ago. Then the curtain fell back into place, like an eyelid over an ephemeral image, only this image—nearly a freeze-frame—the flushed faces, the sweaty brows, the makeup streaked over their wrinkles—didn't vanish at once with the fall of the curtain but persisted on his retina rolling somewhere within him down an endless corridor, and its painful movements he knew at this very moment would be repeated and repeated long afterward.

From the very beginning, reading the simple announcement in the cultural weekly *Free Romania,* he knew that he should remember it, that he would be obliged to remember it, everything about it, in full detail. To remember? What does it mean, to remember, since he had never forgotten it, not one bit, not for a moment? It's true that in time the event suffered some changes in his memory, took on other contours, other significances, but without ever losing clarity of outline, without ever blurring and fading. Quite the contrary.

That morning, in his editorial offices, when he read the announcement, he reconstructed, almost despite himself, the whole senate meeting, as he had never yet done in all those twenty years. Of course, once in a while, some event in his subsequent biography triggered the thought, *there* and *then* in that amphitheater, but he had never summoned up the strength to reconstruct everything. He tried to forget, he forced himself to modify the data of the problem in his mind in such a manner that his guilt (was it his alone?) would lose its sharpness, would blur. Every time, however, there intruded brutally an element of the present that was linked in one way or another to that day, sometimes obliquely and symbolically, but wasn't this sufficient to keep fresh and painful in his mind the memory of that day?

The first years after graduating and being assigned to his job he endeavored to make himself useful, to say yes always, not to think too much, not to ask anything during the meetings, and above all not to ask himself anything. Those were the most peaceful years, when everything went without a hitch: promotions, insignificant appointments to all kinds of committees and commissions, and so forth, until he became a man of importance. Everything was good and became better and better (in fact, he had pushed himself toward this from the time he was a student at the university, as Doina used to point out), up to that moment when the editor responsible for the current issue (Cristian worked at that time for the folklore department) told him, "Comrade Grecu, in two days you have to put together some Christmas carols for the second page, about three or four, but you know, very up-to-date, understand? You'll have to write them and sign them as Ion Stancu, Gică Florea. Choose a typical name as you think best, but it has to sound wholesome, authentic. And put in some villages. Ion Stancu, make him from Cochârlenii-Ilfov. Got it? Come on, everyone, back to work, all of you to work, we don't have time to waste," Georgescu added after calling for the layout editor. Cristian Grecu reentered his office confused. He felt that something was wrong, but in order to clarify things for himself, he'd have to think, and he, Cristian Grecu, had decided since that senate meeting that it wasn't good to think too much because thinking too much would lead him off a precipice, would disorient him, would get him lost. He picked up some sheets of paper and was tapping the table absently with his pen when he caught Anca Ganea glancing at him a little bit amused and a little bit questioning. "And what are you doing? Christmas carols, too?" he asked then, seeing all of them with their noses to the paper. "No, little ducky," said Anca, "only you. You're the only one. We're country children, and Georgescu doesn't dare to ask us to falsify folklore. We told him no, and it's remained no to the end.

But Georgescu knows he has a reliable person, someone he can count on. He knows that among us there's one comrade with great prospects who always says yes, and that means his excesses of zeal (because I don't think anybody could have asked him to produce such an idiotic thing) can be granted substance, thanks to you, as he expects. So, no surprise for us. On the contrary, if you had refused him, we would have wondered, so get on with the job, and 'in the winter's cold the three kings said, we bring you eggs, we bring you bread.'"

Then followed his awakening. A brutal awakening, like that of a boxer, after a few hard punches. Only after that did he realize what had in fact happened years before in that meeting, which almost unwillingly he reconstructed upon reading the announcement in *Free Romania.* . . .

The three of them in the front row of benches. Representatives of the students were customarily placed in the first row of the amphitheater, under the eyes of those who presided. He was the only one who knew what it was about because the first hour of classes that morning, the dean summoned him to his office and told him how pleased he was to have a student like him and that he had a lot of confidence in him and that it would be good for him to speak and to say such and such, the positive things, for example, that the student Andreescu had integrated perfectly and moreover that he had an aptitude for philology and pedagogy, that he would surely make a good teacher, and so on. A good teacher, when Beetle would have been an exceptional film director. . . . During the first days after Beetle joined them, he spoke to nobody. He had a bored air and seemed somehow detached. "An 'angry young man' marooned among us," Doina used to say. Blond, slim, mysterious. Excellently suited for a class with eighty girls. Soon all of them somehow found out that Beetle had participated in a festival of student films in Poland, that the Cinematographic Institute had chosen two films for the festival, but that Beetle had taken with him a third film without approval of any kind, another film made by him (like the other two). Something with some worms, insects, beetles, something symbolic, a parable in short, something "earthshaking." And there in Poland the film was awarded the Grand Prize. This was Beetle's misfortune—the Grand Prize. When he came back home, he said nothing. After a while, the dean received international congratulations for the prizewinning film. How could a film that had not been sent to the festival be awarded a prize? They wondered and wondered and kicked him out. That is to say, Beetle—for his name remained Beetle—and they likewise kicked out the two others who happened to accompany him to the festival. That was more or less the story. The story? The legend? The truth?

Doina and Adrian knew nothing about the day's agenda. The meeting opened with the note of boredom common to all the other meetings the three of them had attended over the course of two years, since their election as representatives of their school year in the senate. At first, they used to participate, with curiosity, and then they became less and less impressed with the grandiloquent and enthusiastic language that no longer amused them at all.

"Comrades," said the dean, at point 4 on the agenda, "we have to discuss the situation of the student Radu Andreescu.

"The student Radu Andreescu was expelled from the Institute of Theatrical and Cinematographic Art in his fourth year of study, following a serious disciplinary violation, but the aforesaid student was vouchsafed the right to reregister in another humanistic faculty as a second-year student, however. We do not focus on the deviation from policy on the basis of which he was expelled. That analysis was made two years ago in the faculty from which the comrade came to us—so it's purposeless for us to waste our time. Student Andreescu reregistered in our university center in the Faculty of Philology, which he has regularly attended and with productive results in learning . . .

"Next," the dean continued, "with the force of the collective and, what's more, with the personal example of other students, Andreescu has been taken back into the fold beyond all expectations, he has even directed small performances here in the faculty, he does not seem to be a disruptive element any longer," and so on.

Cristian Grecu was no longer attentive, the words passed by him as by the others (some of them were nodding off) when he was startled to hear his name. "Cristian Grecu! I grant you the floor in your role as colleague and friend of the student Andreescu and, of course, in your capacity as responsible representative of the student group in which he belongs."

Without the least sense that he was doing any harm (wasn't this true? or—?), Cristian proceeded to repeat all that the dean had "suggested" to him earlier.

"As you've already heard," the dean then contributed, "the student Andreescu is perfectly integrated into the collective in which he belongs; moreover, he has an aptitude for philology. That's why I consider his request that he receive our favorable recommendation for readmittance into the Faculty of Directing, after almost three years of studying philology, to be an immature gesture. Comrades, this is useless now. Why should he return there, if he has proved himself a capable element here? We went so far as to consult with our comrades from the Theatrical Institute and with the comrades from the ministry, who communicated to us that the student Andreescu could even now reenroll in directing but not, of course, without our concurrence. Why, however, should he reenroll there if he is completely integrated here? And more than this, if here he has the chance to continue to direct? By this I mean direction of some programs of sketches, some student performances, he can be in charge of the students' performing brigade. And likewise of the artistic brigades belonging to other faculties, if his time permits."

And the dean again launched forth, he orated with verve, he expatiated, he advanced new arguments, and from time to time, he quoted him, Cristian Grecu, who was (wasn't he?) the one who saw best how profoundly Andreescu was integrated.

"What have you done, old man?" whispered Adrian through his teeth. "You destroyed Beetle with the smile of your lips, praising him. Stand up, stand up now, and tell them that Beetle's vocation is to direct, that directing is his life, that he was born for this."

"I'll stand up myself. I'll tell them everything myself," said Doina.

"It's not you who must do this, but this conscienceless little mouse. He must say it because if it's you, all of them will presume you've been put up to it. He's the one who has to speak. Stand up, man, don't you hear? Don't take away his one chance! On what ground do you claim the right to alter his destiny? For the reward of those filthy fifty one-hundredths of a point which good Young Communists get added to their averages? So you'll have the highest average this year, ahead of Doina and me? For this, man, for this?"

Perhaps the dean's specific words Cristian Grecu didn't remember anymore, but Adrian's whispered words were precisely these.

Then the vote came. Everyone agreed that the student Andreescu must remain in philology (since he's so well integrated), not counting Doina, who abstained, and Adrian, who was against it.

Of course, the dean knew how to raise the issue: Who is in favor of the student Andreescu? Everyone was in favor, being in fact against. Against Beetle's one last chance. Only Adrian Lascu, being against, was actually in favor. Only Adrian had the courage to do what he thought right. Adrian, and, in her way, Doina, who abstained. That was the meeting. Cristian Grecu didn't come across Beetle right afterward. For about a week, Beetle drank continuously. After that he seemed pacified. He was somehow another man. He had been waiting for his chance for three years. And just like that, he lost it. Forever. Now he no longer waited for anything. He had to enter into another character's skin. Enter it forever. That's it, finished with symbols and parables, finished with the Grand Prize, finished with beetles. Indeed, finished. When Cristian Grecu looked for the first time into Andreescu's eyes after that senate meeting— about half a year later, before the exam period in the winter, in the final year—Cristian didn't see in them any reproach, any contempt. No disgust, no fury. His eyes seemed to say, You must give me a new birth, do what you want and how you want with me, let's see what we come out of this with, let's see, *I mean you,* because as for me, I myself won't ever be able to realize anything.

"Excuse me, old man, for keeping you waiting," said Beetle as soon as he returned to the terrace.

In one hand he had a bottle of vodka and in the other, two glasses. He put them on the table, and in the same instant a thick notebook with green vinyl covers dropped from under his arm.

"I made a quick trip up to my room because I wanted to bring you this." He pointed to the notebook with his hand. "Maybe you can find the time to flip through it and see what your friend Andreescu is up to these days."

No, there wasn't the slightest trace of irony in his voice. Maybe just a little emotion, the emotion and the embarrassment of an amateur who asks for the considered judgment of a professional who, by

chance, was a fellow student. A colleague who became a professional while he, Andreescu, took the opposite path. From the Grand
Prize at an international festival to the House of Culture in the little town of M———, where he was amateur stage director and secretary as well as lyricist for the theatrical sketches and had a good
chance to become a manager, maybe eventually a deputy chief of
cultural activities, because the artistic brigade won second place in
the district phase, and the theater team honorable mention at the
national level, and they always give unstinting support and, there
you have it, all's well that ends well.

"Here's my work from the last several years," Andreescu said,
pointing to the notebook with green covers that now lay between
them like a dark sign on the white surface of the table, a boundary
marker, a buoy beyond which and before which were not even
memories, only the present, the concrete and nostalgic present of a
summer evening after twenty years.

It would have been polite for Cristian Greco to reach out and
pick up the notebook and riffle through its pages for a moment,
despite the impossibility of reading it under the natural and invisi-
ble light of the stars. But his hand remained clenched around the
glass of vodka, incapable of movement. From the tips of his fingers
he suddenly felt the chill of the glass penetrate him through and
through (how can you feel cold in June at the simple touch of a
glass?). And it seemed that he should say something, now, not later
(Stand up, stand up now, and tell them, stand up, man, don't take
away his chance!), but his lips were clenched, too, and his teeth, so
tight that the soul itself would not find room to issue forth.

"It's a notebook for directing, in fact there are some character
descriptions, notes on simple people from different workplaces in
M———. I saw them, I interviewed them, I also interviewed their
trade union comrades about them. Thus I have serious and com-
pelling documentation. On this documentary basis, I'll compose the
texts for the brigade and . . ." Andreescu spoke by the book, the sentences were prefabricated, like all the sentences in all the meetings
where no doubt he had said the same things, the same stereotypical
thoughts phrased the same way, with the same for-a-meeting intonation. Yes, Andreescu was what he'd proposed he had to become then,
twenty years ago, after waking up from his drunken stupor. He had

succeeded perfectly, he didn't play, he didn't pretend: he was totally the character he was doomed to be. . . . "Frankly speaking, with this methodology, I don't see how I could miss second place at the national level with my brigade of amateurs. In fact, you'll surely agree with this when you read" (no, there was no longer the faintest trace of the initial shyness of the amateur in the presence of the professional but instead a kind of aplomb acquired over time, the aplomb of one who knows that everyone can produce art and that the professional has a solemn duty to support the amateur, not as a poor or second-rate relative but as a fellow soldier in the cause—something like this could be understood, not from Andreescu's words but from the resoluteness with which he articulated them) "and you'll probably be surprised by the form in which those sketches are arranged. Because they're not simple character sketches but more—in fact, they're small literary pieces, so to speak, you'll see, and then you'll tell me what you think about them. Comrade Ştet himself from the Ministry of Culture saw them, I also showed them to the deputy managing editor for our newspaper, and both of them congratulated me, so that I've already had two highly competent opinions. However, I'd like you to see them yourself. Yes, in the form they are, so as to let you, too, make your own judgment. What do you say?"

Cristian Grecu succeeded in nodding his head yes.

"Then, cheers? To good luck and glory!" said Andreescu, lifting his glass.

"Luck!" Cristian Grecu echoed, and their glasses met above the notebook with green covers, on which a small drop of vodka trickled lazily—a shivering kiss of crystal in the unreal light of the stars.

"Shall we go inside?"

"No, I'd rather stay out here a while."

"OK, I'm going in to chat with some of the others. Who knows when we'll see each other again? Don't forget my notebook here, or you'll ruin me." Beetle pushed the notebook slowly but firmly toward Grecu.

"Don't worry. I'll look it over tonight. Tomorrow morning I'm going to leave at about ten. If I don't run across you, I'll give it to the reception desk to hold for you. Or would you like me to take the notebook with me to Bucharest, to read it more carefully, and to send it back after that?" Grecu heard himself speaking all in one breath, with polished alacrity. It seemed that his feeling of tension had disappeared, and now he used the same studied amiability which he put on anytime when needed or anytime when he had to deal with those who came knocking at the newspaper's door.

"No, old man, don't take it to Bucharest. Not for any reason other than if I don't feel it with me every day, I don't feel like I'm a man. Look over as much of it as you can tonight, and maybe I'll be coming to Bucharest in the autumn because I already ordered some folk costumes from there for the team of dancers, and then we'll see each other and . . . Is that all right?"

"Fine."

As before, Grecu gazed after him as he walked away. Very soon Beetle had to push the curtain aside from the terrace doorway, and in the rectangle of light Grecu would again observe, in a flash, the feverish agitation of the people inside, his fellow students from twenty years ago.

In fact, what did he think? What did he expect Andreescu to be now? A disoriented man? An alcoholic? A sarcastic misanthrope? A shy, withdrawn, disappointed failure who can't find his place? A defeated voice of perpetual lamentation? No. Andreescu was exactly what he decided he would be, what he was forced to decide he would be. A perfectly adapted man. A cultural animator from the provinces, industrious, enterprising, well rooted in reality, a reality accepted with no comments—he left all the comments there in the images of that film from what was now twenty-three years ago. He is what he is, without complexes, without suffering, without irony. He has succeeded.

He lifted the notebook from the table. At the very touch of its covers, he felt, nobody knows why, a wave of bitterness drowning him from his toes up to his head. He had never until now had the concrete evidence, the material proof of the consequences of that senate meeting (of course, Cristian Grecu was overreacting, but on such occasions—which come to people, isn't it so, but once in twenty years?—you have the right to a different kind of sensitivity, if only for a night).

Inside, people were exhausted. Small laughs, the exchange of addresses, promises, empty bottles. The festive little fir tree branches lay wilted on the tables with crumpled napkins and pieces of bread and apple cores. The engineer was staring fixedly at the empty bottle in front of him and seemed to be interested in nothing else. Not even the prospect of becoming a novelist or playwright. He had drunk a lot. And Simu, too. Simu's wife was pale and had teary eyes. At the official table the wife of the deputy dean remained at her seat, dignified and screwed up in her triple chin. All the others were probably scattered now among the former students where, anyhow, it was less boring:

He paid, of course he paid the child support, but he never gave her his name. . . . I think that he'll come back, that's what I think . . . . And I said that they could never reach such a point, and look, they have. . . . With epoxy, with epoxy or with wood glue. . . . You put in three eggs and then add the beaten egg whites. . . . The doctorate? All the cretins have one now. No, sir, better to train as a tailor. . . . No, the wrong doesn't come from there, but it derives from the structure itself. . . . Come on, it's not brick. It's Styrofoam blocks. . . . Elastic? I saw it myself last summer in a fabric shop in Covasna. . . . It isn't possible, they have no weapons, they confiscated the weapons from all of them and all these from the others. . . . What sacrifice, sir? . . . Until when? Until seven o'clock when my mother-in-law goes to take her from the kindergarten. . . . The ultimate purpose is the human being. We must sacrifice everything for the human being. But not the human being himself because we'll fall into mysticism. . . . Of course there's a vaccine, but not for the Asian strain. . . . Two-thirds from the salary, no more. . . . Let sleeping dogs lie, because . . .

For he's a jolly good fellow
For he's a jolly good fellow,
Which nobody can deny . . .

They again raised their glasses and clinked them, kissed each other once more, and again promised to see each other more often because it's such a pity not to.

Cristian Grecu had a room on the second floor, near Simu's. He climbed the stairs (no reason to wait for the elevator for two floors), and when he reached the landing between the first and second floor, he saw at the top of the stairs the silhouette of a woman leaning on the balustrade. When he had climbed until he stood near her, he recognized her. Simu's wife. Her blond hair, which at the beginning of the evening was carefully put up in an elaborate bun, now fell in disarray on her shoulders.

"Can I help you, ma'am?" asked Grecu. The woman turned her head toward him (until then she stood looking over the balustrade) without answering him.

Her big gray eyes, bloodshot because of crying, had the gleam of a young, hungry animal. She stared at him a second, maybe two, after which she turned her face again and was leaning on the balustrade.

The closer Cristian approached the door to his room, the more strongly he felt a mad desire to turn back to take that woman with him for the night, of course she wanted to, at least her eyes said so. . . . But he opened his door, switched on the light, tossed the notebook on the table. If only there's *something* there! If Beetle were still Beetle? If . . . He had no more patience. He opened the notebook. On the first page was the following motto:

> We ever must think, must work, must fight
> To shed on life a glorious light.

Under this motto was written:

> Files for the texts for the arts brigade
>   or
> small, flawed photos on the page
> of a better than perfect age.

On the second page there were some verses followed by a short commentary. He turned some more pages. All had the same structure. He read one at random:

> A worker in our section, Stan,
> Should have been a model man.
> He's industrious, quick, correct.
> But oh, poor Stan has a grave defect.
> He drinks in taverns and at home
> Strong brandy, rum, and beer with foam.
> We've said, out of consideration,

Don't come in such inebriation,
Our collective won't permit at all
A worker who's tippled alcohol.
We tried our best to help and rescue
The once good worker Stan Popescu.
So listen, comrades, don't follow Stan!
Alas, he's not a model man.

After that, there followed a commentary (in prose) on the attitudes and activities (real, concrete, documented) of worker Stan Popescu—from the second section, the machine tool factory in M——. Opinions of fellow workers, of the leader of the trade union group, of his wife.

He read a few more (about deceivers, shirkers, achievers, thieves) and closed the notebook. No, not now, he cannot think about anything now. Tomorrow, to think with a clear mind. Tomorrow in the light. He took a shower—amazing! In this hotel, there was hot water at so late an hour. When he came out from the bathroom, it seemed he could hear someone crying. He pressed his ear to the door. Yes, crying. She was crying. There, on the stairs, Simu's wife. To open the door now, to go up to her, to take her in his arms. Now . . .

In the morning, driving his car on the way back to Bucharest, he surprised himself several times humming the refrain in his mind:

For she's a jolly good fellow,
For she's a jolly good fellow . . .

■ □ ■ □ ■

ABOUT THE AUTHOR

Daniela Crăsnaru won the Romanian Academy Prize, Romania's highest literary honor, in 1991. Before becoming the program director for the Romanian Academy, Rome, she was the general manager at Ion Creangă, Romania's leading publisher of children's books. Her other works include the poetry collections *Sea-Level Zero* and *Letters from Darkness*.

■ □ ■ □ ■

WRITINGS FROM AN UNBOUND EUROPE

For a complete list of titles, see the Writings from an Unbound Europe Web site at
www.nupress.northwestern.edu/ue.